Gently tragic

'He didn't stand a chance. This man . . . he was suddenly behind him. It was over in a moment. He screamed, and fell down . . . It was so vicious. I couldn't believe it. It was like something out of a film.'

A crucial eye-witness records the theatrical unreality of a fatal stabbing in a yuppie backwater of salubrious Kensington, with its gleaming Porsches and sleek Mercedes, a stone's throw from the flat of Detective Chief Superintendent George Gently and his wife, Gabrielle.

A hunting knife protrudes from the back of Stan Reydon, tough, successful businessman and habitually unfaithful husband.

Sex, business dealings, hatred and revenge – a dramatic mix of powerful emotions is patiently sifted as, one by one, Reydon's closest private and professional relationships come under Gently's expert scrutiny.

An embittered wife; a flamboyant, unstable mistress; a cuckolded husband; an employee dismissed for dishonesty; another now a jobless widower with a life-long grudge – their actions and alibis are minutely explored.

As the pressure of the murder hunt mounts, a persistent, anonymous, croaky voice – a voice that has been out in the rain – goads Gently in a series of tantalizing 'phone calls, pointing the finger . . .

The deductive powers, intuitive inspiration, integrity and compassion of his famous creation, George Gently, are all manifest in this, Alan Hunter's fortieth novel of suspense.

Other murder cases investigated by Chief Superintendent Gently, CID.

GENTLY TRAGIC

Alan Hunter

Constable · London

First published in Great Britain 1992
by Constable & Company Limited
3 The Lanchesters, 162 Fulham Palace Road, London W6 9ER
Copyright © 1992 by Alan Hunter
The right of Alan Hunter to be
identified as the author of this work
has been asserted by him in accordance
with the Copyright, Designs and Patents Act 1988
ISBN 0 09 471700 1
Set in Linotron 11pt Palatino
and printed in Great Britain by
Redwood Press Limited
Melksham, Wiltshire

A CIP catalogue record for this book
is available from the British Library

The characters and events in this book are
fictitious; the locale is sketched from life.

1

A sudden, inexplicable explosion of tragedy, in the midst of life, freezes pity; and even resentment. At the touch of a switch, reality has changed and we are jerked into a different world.

It had been a familiar enough world that evening. At the Yard it had been a slow day, and in the afternoon I had rung Gabrielle and suggested a visit to a show she had wanted to see. We had met at her favourite restaurant, off Leicester Square, and gone on from there to the theatre. The show was no great matter, but in the bar at the interval she had run into her bosom friend, Julia Mannering, and her husband, Reg, and they came to sit with us afterwards, and shared a drink after the show. Then they went on to a night-club, and we caught a taxi back to Lime Walk.

'Oh dear, that gown Julia was wearing!'

Yes, she had needed the fur wrap her husband had held out for her. The sleet of late November had held up, but the temperature couldn't have been far off freezing.

Above the city lights, the lights of traffic, hung a pitch black sky that held a hint of snow.

'I shall make coffee – and then to bed!'

Surprisingly, the taxi was quite well heated. Gabrielle snuggled up in my arm contentedly, sat watching the traffic, the streets roll by. We reached Kensington, the Church Street, and then we heard a police siren sounding behind us. It drew closer. After a pause, our driver slowed and drew in to the pavement.

'It is an ambulance, perhaps?'

'No. A patrol car.'

A moment later it swooped past us. Then its brake lights flashed, it signalled, and turned down towards Lime Walk.

'My dear – can something have happened?'

Our taxi continued and made the same turn. We came to the Walk, dull, poorly lit, still shadowed by the few trees to have escaped the hurricane.

'It has stopped near ours!'

Its light was flashing, stationary, towards the far end of the Walk. There we could dimly see one or two people standing round something, a black shadow on the pavement. Gabrielle gripped my arm very hard.

'Pull in here. Behind the patrol car.'

The black shadow was a body and pooling blood. It lay only yards from the entrance to our flat.

'Stay in the taxi.'

'But –!'

I jumped out and slammed the door behind me. One of the patrolmen was in the car, radioing in, the other stood trying to take in what he was seeing.

'Chief Superintendent Gently. All of you stay back! Did anyone see what happened here?'

'Yes. I did!'

It was an elderly lady who occupied a flat across the way from ours.

'I was putting the milk out – I heard him scream. Oh my God, it was terrible.'

'Did you see who did it?'

'Yes – someone. I shouted something, and he ran. But I

6

couldn't see who. He was just a dark figure. He ran into the mews. Then I came in and dialled 999.'

'Into the mews.' I nodded to the patrolman, who came out of his stupor and galloped off up the alley. 'Did anyone else here see anything?' I stared round at the bystanders. They were mostly residents whom I recognized.

'Yes. We did.'

He was a stocky, city-dressed man with a neat beard. I had seen him before, but I didn't know his name. A woman was hanging on his arm, her face averted.

'Where were you?'

'Never mind me! That fellow down there is this lady's husband.'

'Her husband. Then she was with him?'

'No. But she saw what bloody happened.'

The woman burst into tears. She clung to the man's arm. A woman of around forty, in a severe black suit. She, too, I had seen before: a recent addition to the Lime Walk scene. She was doing her best to halt her tears, was fishing in her handbag for a tissue. To the man, I said:

'So tell me what you saw.'

'I was down the other end, outside my house. I'd just stepped out for a breath of air. Anthea came by. I said good-evening to her.'

'Anthea?'

'Mrs Reydon! That's him down there, with the hole in his back. She was hurrying to catch him up, he was about half-way up the Walk.'

'Oh God!' the woman sobbed. 'Let me tell it, Phil. Stanley was dining with a client this evening. I went down to Bertie's Hotel for a drink, then I saw Stan as I was coming back. I hurried to catch him, but he got here first – this is our house, we've only just moved here. And suddenly this man came out from behind the tree and struck Stan in the back.' She gulped down a sob.

7

'How far away were you?'

'I don't know! Perhaps fifty yards.'

'And the man?'

'I never saw his face. He looked huge. He was wearing a dark coat.'

'No one known to you?'

'Oh God, no. It was like someone out of a nightmare.'

'I saw him too,' the man said. 'Only I was further away. I'd put him at six feet, and dressed in dark clothes, like Anthea says.'

'You saw him strike . . . Reydon?'

'I saw him. And Stan screamed, and I began running. But the sod had cleared off, and Stan lay there bleeding, with the handle of that knife sticking out of his back.'

Yes: the knife. Now it lay on the pavement, alongside the outstretched body. A hunting knife with a horn handle with part of the horn on the upper side missing.

'It was you who pulled it out?'

'Did you expect me to leave it in? Yes, I pulled it out. He could still have been alive when I got here.'

'But he wasn't.'

'He bloody wasn't.'

'How long ago when this happened?'

'Twenty minutes at the most. I was going into Anthea's to ring the police, but this lady came out and told us she'd already done it.'

'Did you see anyone else around when it happened?'

'No. Just him and us. And the bloke.'

I looked around. 'Any other witnesses?'

A shuffling of feet, but no takers. I went to take a closer look at the body. It was that of a man in his mid-forties, solidly built, his ginger hair in a style. He was wearing a baggy shell suit, which seemed odd for a man who'd been dining out with a client. He had boyish, snub-nosed fea-

8

tures. The knife had gone in under the left shoulder-blade. The patrolman returned.

'No one about there, sir.'

'Ring in his description. Six feet, big build, wearing a dark or black coat.'

I'd forgotten the taxi. Gabrielle was paying it off. Then there were sirens and a clanging ambulance bell.

And suddenly it had the air of a fête or a sporting event, out there on the dimly lighted Walk, with more and more of the residents, known or half-known, hastening to join the silent bystanders. There were four police cars now, with the ambulance towering over them, and uniform men holding the ring while the police surgeon, Latham, knelt by the body. Gabrielle held my arm. She wouldn't go in. In fact, this affair was taking place on our doorstep. The alley to the mews and three doors were all that separated our flat from the fatal spot.

'My dear . . . I have spoken to that man.'

'To . . . ?'

Gabrielle nodded. 'That red Porsche belongs to him. Last week, I am setting out to shop when he is coming down the steps and getting in his car. Hallo, he says, we are going to be neighbours, one evening you must come round for a drink. And in his eyes is a wicked look. And he eyes me up and down.'

'You would say he was a wolf?'

'But yes. A wolf. And the poor lady his wife, I am seeing her often. But she, she has no wish to make my acquaintance. I would say her life has not been a happy one.'

'And the man she is with?'

'Once, he has visited her, when the red Porsche is not outside. But I do not think . . . you know? Always, she is dressing like some person's secretary.'

9

I looked at the lady with more interest. Certainly, she wasn't dressed to kill. Under the severe two-piece, a woolly jumper; with drab stockings and sensible shoes.

Now she had separated from the bearded man, though she remained standing close to him. She was watching the proceedings with wretched eyes, her mouth in a thin hoop. Forty? Forty-two? Just the hint of a figure under all that disguise. Straight black hair and no jewellery. Some person's secretary summed her up.

'He calls her Anthea.'

'Ha. But all the same, I do not think.'

Latham got up and came over. 'Got him square in the left ventricle.'

'He would have died instantly?'

'Very instantly. And the odds are your man will have some blood on him. Should I give the widow a shot?'

'I doubt if it's necessary.'

Latham nodded. 'She looks like a lady who's got it all together.'

He climbed into a car and left. More people were arriving all the time. Subtly, the feel of the affair was still changing, was becoming almost party-like in atmosphere. Everyone here knew everyone else, by sight if not by acquaintance, and the initial silence was thawing. Now and then there was even a smothered guffaw. Yet stark and plain the body lay there, the pooled blood, the knife. It awaited the photographer. Slowly, its reality seemed draining away. Then another car drew up, and the lanky figure of Chief Inspector Tanner climbed out.

He stood a moment, staring. Then he saw me, and came over.

'Well, well! And on your doorstep too, sir. That chummie just has to be an amateur.'

'We arrived here shortly after it happened.'

'It gets better. Were there any witnesses?'

10

'Three people.'

'Only three? I'm beginning to feel sorry for this geezer.'

'Unfortunately their descriptions are rather vague.'

'Never mind, sir. Memories often improve.'

Tanner was the local CID chief: in his hands the investigation rested. I gave him a brief narrative of what had passed since we arrived. At once he dispatched two men to the mews to give them a second, more systematic, search, and confirmed that patrols, equipped with that vague description, were cruising the streets into which chummie may have fled.

'But if he's got into the flipping park . . .'

Holland Park lay just beyond the Walk. On a thought, Tanner extended the alert area to streets bounding that wide expanse.

Next, the photographers came, and once more the mood suffered a change. People crowded round as close as they were permitted to watch them set up and arrange their shots. No thought of silence now! The body had been reduced to a problem of angles. Three yuppies, arriving from some carouse, mistook the proceedings for a film set, and their jeering cries had to be subdued by a harsh warning from Tanner's sergeant, Edith.

'And this is what happens . . . all the time . . . for you?'

Still Gabrielle was cuddling my arm. She was watching everything with large eyes, and now and then the pressure on my arm tightened.

'Not all the time.'

'But . . . often?'

'It becomes a matter of routine. Why don't you go in now?'

'Oh no. If you must stay, then so will I.'

The photographers finished. Then it was the turn of the ambulance men with their stretcher. Though they did their best to be expeditious, they had some trouble with the weighty corpse. Also it was still warm, the arms persisted in flopping loose from the stretcher: they were obliged to strap them in before covering the corpse and carting it away. At this point the widow had turned her back and buried her face in the bearded man's chest.

'Thurloe – Cresswell. Fetch some water and clean this bloody lot up!'

Tanner himself had secured the knife, edging it into a plastic bag. He brought it to show me.

'Look at this, sir.'

On the handle remained a stick-on price label. Now bloodied and soiled, it yet had the appearance of being new.

'If we can trace this, sir, we'll perhaps get a description we can use. If you ask me I'd say it could be a mugging. The boyo had plenty of cash in his wallet.'

'It didn't sound like a mugging.'

'I don't know, sir. Rush of blood and all that. Then he hears the lady sing out and takes off before he can pick up the dough.'

I shook my head. 'Would you know the victim?'

'I know most people on my patch, sir. Reydon Contracts, that's who he is. You'll see his office in the Church Street.'

'Reydon Contracts . . . ?'

'Don't ask me what he did, sir. Just something in the building line is all I know.'

From somewhere the two DCs had found a bucket and a broom and the last act in the tragedy was proceeding. Blood, even fresh blood, sticks, and a good deal of scrubbing was needed here. The bucket went back and forth to the mews. Pink water flooded down the gutter to the drain. Finally the pavement was clean, and a last bucket of water thrown down.

'Now, madam – I'm sorry to have to ask you this. And

you, sir. And the lady who gave us the ring. I must ask you to come along to the station and get you to give me your signed statements.'

'But you can't do that!' The bearded man's head jerked. 'Can't you see that Mrs Reydon is in a state of shock?'

'Mr Lampard, is it?'

'Yes – Lampard!'

'Then I'm sorry, sir. But this does happen to be a case of homicide.'

'But we told that man all we saw.'

'I'm sorry, sir. But that's how it goes.'

'But it would do in the morning.'

'Sorry, sir. We need you to make those statements while it's all still fresh.'

'And if we refuse?'

Mrs Reydon laid a fluttering hand on his arm. 'It's all right, Phil. He's only doing his duty. It's best if we get it over with now.'

'But you're in shock, Anthea!'

Mrs Reydon shuddered. 'I'm alive, Phil. And Stan is dead. And he didn't deserve that. Whatever we can do to help catch that man, we should do.'

'That's the way to look at it, ma'am,' Tanner said. 'And I can promise you we won't keep you long. And if you don't fancy staying here alone tonight I'll have a WPC come back with you.'

Mrs Reydon shook her head. 'Then . . . if we may go?'

Lampard wanted to say something, but bit his tongue. The third witness, a Mrs Cartwright, went to fetch her handbag. Tanner signalled for a car. Mrs Cartwright returned. And then the scene took a different turn entirely.

'Where is he? Where's Stan!'

A furious woman came thrusting through the crowd. She

13

saw Tanner. She threw herself upon him. She beat on his chest with clenched fists.

'Ma'am!'

'Where is he – where is he?'

'Ma'am –!'

'Tell me what you bastards have done with him! Is he dead?'

'Please – ma'am!'

'I want to know what you've done with Stan!'

She was a bold-figured, fluffy blonde clad in a *risqué* dress and a flapping swagger-coat, her eyes blazing and smudged make-up on her lank cheeks and thin lips. She whimpered.

'It was him – wasn't it? The bloke who they said was knifed up here! That's what all this is about – they've gone and done poor Stan in.'

'Ma'am, you are –'

'Who do you think!'

'Perhaps, if you could just cool down a little –'

'Bloody why should I cool down, when those sods have done him in! Where is he?'

'If you mean Mr Reydon –'

'Stan. Stan!'

'– all that's being taken care of. And now, if you don't mind –'

The lady screamed. She had just caught sight of the shrinking Lampard and his companion, who had been lurking behind Tanner's car, seemingly doing their best to escape observation. Now, every eye turned in their direction.

'So the bastard's here – right here!'

'Ma'am –'

'Look – he's here. Not in the office where he said he'd be.'

'Ma'am –'

'And look who's with him. Little Mrs Butter-wouldn't-

14

melt! If you ask me she was in it with him – she was supposed to be out somewhere, too.'

She stalked menacingly towards the pair. Hastily, Lampard got in front of Mrs Reydon.

'Now listen, Sara –'

'Murderer!'

'Sara, will you listen!'

'Murderer! You killed him, you bastard. It was all a trick, you being at the office.'

'I'd just got back –'

'Liar!'

'Yes, I'd just got out of my car. Anthea can tell you –'

'Anthea nothing. You worked this together, you bastards.'

'Here, here, here!' Tanner rumbled. 'If you've anything to say, you say it to me, lady. Am I to take it you are this gentleman's wife, and that you've something to tell me about this evening?'

'Oh yes, you bet I have!'

'Sara, for God's sake!' Lampard pleaded.

'I'll tell him,' she snarled. 'Oh yes, I'll tell him. This is the end between you and me, bloody Phil Lampard. Now it's all cards on the table.'

'Sara, please!'

Sara Lampard turned to Tanner. 'You want to know where poor Stan was this evening – when my husband was supposed to be kept at the office, and that bitch was supposed to be out at her mother's?'

'Sara!'

'He was with me. He was with me back at the house. In my bedroom. On the bed. If you want me to go on, just say the word.'

'You shameless bitch!' Mrs Reydon hissed.

'You know what he called you,' Sara Lampard jeered. 'Little Mrs Butter-won't-melt. And he told me why. So chew on that.'

'You cow!'

'You frigid mare.'

'You're no better than a tart!'

'And you're not as good.'

'Will you two belt up?' Tanner bawled. 'In a minute I'll be running you in for disturbing the peace.'

But it was too late. What had started as tragedy was switching now into farce. The yuppies hooted, women were giggling, and another couple had started an argument on the fringe of the gathering. A farce: with Mrs Reydon looking anything but a woman whose husband's body had just been carted away.

'Officer, this woman is a slanderous liar!'

'Just tell them when you last slept with Stan!'

'She is notorious. Ask her husband.'

'Last Easter, was it?'

'Filth. You're filth!'

'You tell her, girl!' hooted a yuppie. 'I know which one I would rather sleep with.'

It was getting out of hand. Tanner glanced at Edith.

'Right – you two beauties are under arrest! And either you come quietly or you don't, but whichever way, you're going to come.'

Edith shaped up beside Sara Lampard. Tanner bore down on Mrs Reydon.

'But – but you can't do this!' Lampard spluttered, thrusting himself between them. Tanner glared at him.

'In your case it'll be cuffs. Now get in that car along with the lady.'

'But –'

'Get in that car!'

With a dignity that was comic, Lampard got in. Mrs Reydon hastened in after him, and Tanner banged the car, which accelerated away. Edith's task wasn't so simple. Sara Lampard had planted her feet defiantly. When Edith took

16

her elbow she jumped back, stood daring him with wide, mascaraed eyes.

'If you touch me again, I'll have you!'

'Bring a car up!' Tanner bawled.

The car came. Together with Edith, Tanner crowded the screeching Sara Lampard into it, to be followed by an unfortunate DC, whom I saw later with plaster on his cheek.

'Shame!' a yuppie shouted. 'We'll see you when you come out, darling!'

Tanner gave his bang and the car left: with the yuppies running down the pavement beside it. Tanner faced the crowd.

'All right! Now the fun and games are over. So I'm ordering you lot to disperse peacefully and go about your business. Understood?'

They understood, but still were reluctant to break up the party. However, the more respectable element began to melt away, and uniform men drifted towards the others.

'Do you still – want me?'

The elderly Mrs Cartwright stood forgotten in the background, still clutching her bag, a dazed expression in her eyes. Tanner apologized and packed her into a car. The kindly Edith went with her. Then, after gazing a moment, Tanner turned to me.

'Sir, I could use a bloody drink!'

The silent flat seemed odd, misplaced, so close to the scene breaking up outside. We sat Tanner down in the lounge and I poured him a scotch, while a silent Gabrielle heated coffee in the kitchen. I poured myself one. We sat sipping. The clock said it had turned one. We had barely finished our drinks when Gabrielle returned with a tray.

'Sugar?'

'Make it two, ma'am.'

They were the first words to be spoken. And it was not until Tanner had sampled what was certainly the best coffee in Kensington that he added:

'Around six foot, in dark clothing. What do you make of it, sir?'

I paused for a sip from my own cup. 'Check, check and check again.'

'Don't worry – I'll be doing that! But you think there's a chance we're on to a juicy one?'

I drank. 'What do we know about him?'

'Same line of business as Reydon,' Tanner said. 'He's a builder's supplier, with his yard in the Bush – Hagg Lane, is where I think he hangs out.'

'His office is there?'

'Right.'

'His first tale was that he'd just stepped out for some air.'

'And the lady. Fresh back from Bertie's.'

I drank. 'So check. And check again.'

Gabrielle had brought her coffee to sit by me. She stared very solemnly at Tanner. She said:

'I am watching this man and this woman, and I do not think it is, what you call, juicy.'

'She seemed all over him to me, ma'am.'

'Ha. But is that not to be expected? She has just seen what she has seen, and will she not be clinging to any person who is known to her? I think so. I am watching them closely. They may be confederates, but it is no more.'

Tanner shook his head. 'Not that it matters, ma'am, if what the other lady says is right. They'd be in it together, setting it up, and her perhaps egging him on, if he needed it.'

'That other lady has a guilty conscience.'

'I am much of your opinion, ma'am. So we'll just see where it leads us, perhaps with a little grain of salt.'

Gabrielle made a face. I said:

18

'Do we know if Lampard had business dealings with Reydon?'

'Ah.' Tanner drank coffee. 'That's a line we shall have to follow up, sir. But it's the other one I like. And I think it's the one that's going to stick. It only needs us to find that chummie wasn't at the office, and then we shall be in business.'

'It still might run deeper than a cheating wife.'

'Could be a secondary motive, sir. But then again, we could be dealing with a mugger, and all this comic stuff just on the side.'

He finished his coffee, and refused a second cup. Outside now all was quiet. Tanner rose. He said:

'I know it's a bit of cheek, sir, but you were on the job before I got here.'

'You want me along?'

'If the missus doesn't mind. Just to sit in while we take these statements.'

'Ha, this I am expecting,' Gabrielle said. 'And if this mugger is still lurking about here?'

'Not to worry, ma'am!' Tanner said hastily. 'My men will be outside all night.'

'This you swear?'

'It's routine, ma'am.'

Gabrielle cast me a doleful look. 'Then, George Gently, do not wake me up, when you arrive back home in the small hours!'

I kissed her, and we left. Lime Walk was deserted except for policemen. Few windows were lit, and the house was dark beside the pale patch that showed on the pavement. A patrol car waited; I briefly paused before climbing in after Tanner. Was it real, what had happened here, in this place which, in London, we called home? Something – however temporarily – had changed, in Lime Walk.

19

2

In a corner of Tanner's office I sat down to scribble my statement, all I had seen and been told in those first hectic moments in Lime Walk.

Tanner, meanwhile, had dispatched a DC to Bertie's Hotel, and rung the CID at Shepherd's Bush for a check to be made at Hagg Lane.

Then Mrs Cartwright was fetched in, still with a dazed look in her eyes. With her came Mary, one of the WPCs, to squat by the desk with her pad and pencil. Tanner had ordered mugs of tea to be brought, and Mrs Cartwright sipped hers tremblingly. I was still scribbling when Tanner said, very gently:

'Now, ma'am. If you'll just tell us what you saw?'

She did her best. Always, at that time, she put out her milk-basket for the morning, after making a cup of chocolate to take in with her to bed. She'd been watching a thriller on TV, and had put the kettle on when it ended. Then, as she'd opened her door, milk-basket in hand, she'd caught sight of the new man across the road, a few steps from his house.

'Coming up the Walk, ma'am?'

'Yes, up the Walk.'

'Would you have noticed anything unusual about him?'

'Anything . . . ?'

'In his demeanour, ma'am. Like was he in a hurry, maybe giving a glance back over his shoulder.'

Mrs Cartwright looked worried. 'I . . . don't think so. But I wasn't giving him much attention. Perhaps he was walking rather quickly, but I couldn't say any more than that.'

'Rather quickly,' Tanner said, and Mary scuffed it down. Tanner said: 'And further down the Walk, ma'am. Would you have noticed anyone along there?'

'No. Nobody.'

'A man? A woman?'

'No. I didn't come out of my porch. I could only see across the road, just the house and his car parked there.'

'Were there lights in the house?'

'I didn't notice.'

'But he seemed in a hurry.'

'Perhaps . . . yes.'

Tanner sighed softly. He said: 'Now ma'am, in your own words. What happened next?'

Mrs Cartwright's hands were fluttering. She was staring at Tanner with helpless eyes.

'He – he had just got past the car. There's that tree there that wasn't blown down. It's away from the street light, and makes a lot of shadow, and just there, as he turned towards his steps . . .'

'Take it easy, ma'am!' Tanner murmured.

'Yes . . . just there, as he was turning.'

'He had his back to the fellow?'

She nodded. 'He didn't stand a chance. This man . . . he was suddenly behind him. It was over in a moment. He screamed, and fell down.'

'The man had been behind the tree.'

'Yes.'

'The one blow.'

She closed her eyes. 'It was . . . so vicious. I – I couldn't believe it. It was like something out of a film.'

'And – you shouted?'

'I couldn't help it.'

'And this fellow bolted?'

'Yes. And I dropped the milk-basket and slammed the door.'

'And you rang us.'

She nodded.

'How soon after?'

'As soon as I could pull myself together. I don't know! Then I looked through the window, and saw that man and that woman standing beside . . . him.'

'You mean Mr Lampard and Mrs Reydon.'

'I didn't know it was his wife.'

'What were they doing?'

'Nothing . . . staring. Then some other people ran up. So I went out too. Then the police car came. And Mr Gently, in a taxi.'

Tanner snapped and unsnapped a ballpen. Mary's pencil skittered over her pad. Mrs Cartwright stared at the desk: but clearly it wasn't what she was seeing. Tanner said:

'This man.'

Her eyes jumped to his.

'Would you call him tall?'

'I . . . yes.'

'About the same height as Mr Reydon?'

'Perhaps . . . yes. But he was bigger.'

'How – bigger?'

'To me he seemed . . . it may have been the coat he was wearing. It was black, or a dark colour. He looked enormous. Like a man out of a nightmare.'

'Would you have seen his face?'

She shuddered. 'He never looked in my direction. When I shouted he simply ran off, up that alley into the mews.'

22

'Did you notice his hair?'

She shook her head.

'Is there anything else you can tell us about him?'

But there wasn't. Brave little Mrs Cartwright had shot her bolt. She went off with Mary to be found a car to take her back to her cold cup of chocolate. An offer of a companion for the rest of the night was turned down with dignity; and, on leaving, she gave me a look that would have been a smile, if she could have raised one.

Some of the fire had gone out of Sara Lampard, but she had had time to repair her make-up. Her lank face had a sulky expression as she was escorted into the office. By now, I had joined Tanner at the desk. She swept us with a glance of calculated disdain. Then she sat on the chair provided for her and made a deliberate display of crossing her legs. She said:

'So what do you want to know that you don't know?'

'Do make yourself comfortable, ma'am,' Tanner said.

'I am bloody comfortable. So what do you want to know that I haven't told you already?'

Tanner glanced at me. I said: 'I'm sure you know what we want, Mrs Lampard. Regrettably, we require the details of the events that took place this evening. Only when we have them will there be a chance of our arresting the person who killed your friend, for which, I assume, you are as concerned as ourselves.'

She stared at me meanly. 'What do you care about Stan?'

I stared back, said: 'Perhaps it's more a question of how much you cared about him.'

'Me! What the hell do you mean by that?'

'For example, were you intending to leave your husband?'

'Oh, that.' Her mouth twisted. 'Maybe yes, and maybe

23

no. But I wasn't aiming to run off with Stan, so you can put that idea out of your head. We were just good friends. He swung a contract for Phil, and we had a celebration supper at Bertie's. That's where I met him. I liked his style. We've had a few more celebrations since. But that's about it. I'll be leaving bloody Phil because he's a bastard, and can be violent.'

'Violent . . . ?'

'Yes, the sod. He's given me a black eye before now.'

'Because there have been other men?'

She slanted me a look. 'Never you mind about that.'

I said: 'Then let's get back to this evening. There's no question that Mr Reydon spent it with you.'

'I told you, didn't I?'

Mary's pencil began to rustle, and Sara Lampard flicked her a malignant stare.

'It was you who arranged it?'

'If you say so. Bloody Phil rang me from the office. He said he had a quote to get out for a job at Staines, and I needn't expect him back till past eleven. So that was me with a blank evening, and not a damn thing worth seeing on the telly. I gave Stan a tinkle. He told me that little Mrs Butter was spending the evening with her mother in Chiswick.'

'With her mother?'

'That's what the bitch told him.'

'Go on.'

'Well, that's how it was. Stan went home to check that she'd really pissed off. Then he came on to mine, and I fed him a meal, and what happened after that is no business of yours. It went on a bit. I wanted him to go, but he said his wife never got back before midnight. At last, at eleven, I had to toss him out. And then I put some coffee on and waited for Phil.'

'Who didn't turn up.'

24

'You know he bloody didn't! In the end I came out to look for his car. And that's when I saw what was going on up there' – her mouth twisted – 'and some bugger told me that Stan had been knifed.'

'And, at once, you assumed –?'

'I was bloody certain!' She choked a sob in her voice. 'That bastard said he'd do the next one an injury – and there he was, standing there, with that frigid bitch hanging on to him. It was all set up. He was never at the office, and she was never over at Chiswick.'

I said: 'Your husband threatened to do your next lover an injury?'

'Yes – write it down, write it down! Some rotten bitch shopped me to him another time, and that's when he gave me a black eye.'

'And Mr Reydon was – the next one?'

'Yes he was – well, at least as far as Phil was concerned.'

'You'd been shopped again?'

'Must have been. Or it could have been little Mrs Butter kept an eye on him.' She dabbed her eyes, which were smeary again. 'Anyway, you've got him. You've bloody got him. So he won't be knocking me about, and when he gets out I shall be long gone.'

'You intend leaving him?'

'Are you kidding, sunshine? Wouldn't you say I had grounds for a divorce now?'

I said: 'I think you perhaps shouldn't jump to conclusions, Mrs Lampard. We have no grounds for charging anyone yet.'

Her eyes were big. 'No bloody grounds?'

I shook my head. 'We shall, of course, require your husband to account for his movements but, for the moment, there is no charge against him.'

'But he did it!'

'We may not assume that at this stage of the enquiry.'

'You mean' – she gave a gasp – 'you mean you could let him out again?'

I paused, then simply nodded.

'Oh my God!' She snatched her eyes away. 'That bastard. He'll kill me too.'

'We shall, of course, admonish him to keep the peace, or face immediate arrest.'

'But what good is that, after he's knocked me cold? No, bloody no. I shall have to clear out, mate.' She stared at me painfully. 'How long have I got?'

'Your husband will not be released just yet.'

'But how long! I've got to pack a bag.'

I shrugged. 'I think you will have time to do that.'

'Then – can I go?'

I looked at Tanner. 'OK by me, sir,' Tanner said. 'Just as soon as she signs her statement. Mary, get it typed up right away.' He cocked a look at Sara Lampard. 'Where shall we find you, ma'am, if we want you?'

'I'll be at Bertie's – but don't tell that sod!'

'Just as long as we know, ma'am,' Tanner said.

Sara Lampard departed in haste after the expressionless Mary, and Tanner gave me a knowing wink. But before he could speak the phone rang: Shepherd's Bush was calling back. Tanner listened, made a note, hung up.

'So that's that, sir,' he said. 'Lampard's alibi has gone for a Burton. They've talked to the night-watchman, and Lampard left the office at half five.'

And at once there was a tap on the door, and the DC who'd been sent to Bertie's entered. He said:

'No go, sir. They know the lady quite well there, but they don't remember seeing her there last night.'

'Well, well,' Tanner said. 'Well, well. It gets more interesting by the minute.'

Mary returned from typing Sara Lampard's statement, and then Philip Lampard was ushered in. He stood perhaps under six feet but otherwise fitted the description we had quite well. He had a sturdy, broad-shouldered build and wore a black three-quarter coat over a pin-striped black business suit. Seen from behind, in the dim light of a street lamp, he might well have made the figure described by Mrs Cartwright.

He had greying, thinning hair and angry brown-hazel eyes, and wide-cheekboned features narrowing to a sharp chin and the small beard. He came in abruptly, and took the chair placed for him without being asked. He gave me a fierce stare, then deliberately turned his gaze on Tanner. At once I could see Tanner bristling. He snapped his ballpen once or twice. He said:

'Just before we begin your statement, Mr Lampard! I understand it was you who pulled the knife out. Would you like to explain why you did that?'

Lampard's beard jerked. 'What the devil else would you expect? If the fellow was to have a chance, it wasn't with a knife sticking out of his back.'

'It was just for – humanitarian reasons?'

'What are you trying to say?'

'Just this, Mr Lampard. There were someone's finger-prints on that knife, but the only prints on it now are yours.'

Lampard stared. 'Well – I can't help that!'

'But you could have helped it,' Tanner said. 'A moment earlier you'd seen that knife in the hand of the killer, so you couldn't have not known whose prints were on it.'

'But I didn't think!'

'You didn't?'

'No. I just did the natural thing.'

'The natural thing,' Tanner said. 'Like destroying vital evidence. Like that.' He snapped his pen. 'We might have known them,' he said. 'Those prints may have been on record at the Yard. They might have matched other prints. Like the prints of someone present at the scene.'

'I tell you, I'm sorry!'

'While all we have now are your prints. Overlaying the killer's prints. Just yours.'

Did he know what Tanner was getting at? If so, he concealed it pretty well. His expression was of mingled exasperation and bafflement. Only the play of his hands revealed an undercurrent of uneasiness.

'All right,' Tanner said, softly. 'We'll leave that. Perhaps we can come back to it later. What we need from you now, Mr Lampard, is an account of your movements last night. Let's say from the time your office packed up.'

'My movements!' Lampard jerked straight. 'Surely you don't believe those accusations of Sara's? Why –'

'Just your movements,' Tanner said. 'From five thirty, Mr Lampard.'

Now the hands were really revealing. Lampard looked from Tanner to me, and back to Tanner. At last he said sulkily:

'I remained at my office until eleven.'

'At your office,' Tanner said.

'Yes.'

'With the lights on,' Tanner said.

'Of course with the lights on!'

Tanner shook his head. 'I think you'd better sack that night-watchman of yours,' he said. 'He must be blind or somewhere near it. He claims he never saw a thing.'

'But – perhaps he wouldn't have seen me!'

'What – not in the office?'

'No. I had the blinds drawn.'

'Then there'd be the cleaning lady,' Tanner pondered. 'I suppose you do have one. What's her name?'

'I – I went out for a meal!' Lampard faltered.

'Must have been a long meal,' Tanner said. 'From five

thirty right through till eleven. Going to make the *Guinness Book of Records*, that one.'

'I mean, while the cleaner was in the office!'

'So like that, no one saw you at all.'

'No – it's possible.'

'Not a soul to vouch for you. From five thirty p.m. till . . . when was it?'

The hands – they were large ones – doubled into fists. 'Once and for all, I was at the office!'

'I hear you telling me,' Tanner said. 'At the office. So now we get back to the knife.'

Lampard's face was red, his stare helpless, thick lips parted over uneven teeth. For a moment he hung on, breathing heavily. Then he jumped to his feet.

'I want my solicitor!'

'Please sit down, Mr Lampard.'

'No. I won't answer any more questions, except in my solicitor's presence.'

'Now, you wouldn't want us to think –'

'I was at my office, and that's all I'm saying.'

'But you can't deny that, after –'

'I tell you, I'm not saying another word.'

I said: 'We need your statement, Mr Lampard, and your solicitor may not be immediately available. You made a statement to me at the scene which there can be no harm in your repeating now.'

He glared at me. 'I refuse!'

'A refusal is liable to be misinterpreted.'

'I don't care. I'm saying no more.'

'Then, at least sit down again on your chair.'

With an ill grace, he complied. I nodded to Tanner. Tanner followed me out of the office. Outside, he gave me a rueful look, said:

'Sorry, sir! I made a balls-up of that one. What do we do?'

29

I said: 'Take a risk. We'll have the widow and him in together.'

Tanner sucked in breath. 'Do you think it will work?'

'If it doesn't, then the can stops with me.'

A fresh chair was placed, alongside Lampard's, and Mrs Reydon was fetched by a WPC. She hesitated on seeing Lampard, then hastened to take her seat beside him. A look passed between them, her eyes fraught, his frowning and uncertain. Then she tidied her skirt deftly and applied her gaze to me. Tanner sat. I sat. Mary flicked over a leaf of her pad and scribbled something. I said:

'This shouldn't take long, Mrs Reydon, but you will appreciate that we do need your statement. Just a few details to begin with. When did you last see your husband, before tonight?'

'When? Oh, at lunch.' She spoke with determined self-possession.

'And he seemed quite normal?'

'Oh yes. He was just the same as always.'

'And you mentioned your plans for the evening to him?'

'My plans?' She darted a quick glance at Lampard.

'Your plan of visiting your mother at Chiswick. It was mentioned to us by another witness.'

'But –!' The self-possession was fading.

'You don't have to answer him!' Lampard snapped. 'They've been talking to Sara, of course, and you can guess what she's been telling them.'

'But if they know –'

'They don't know anything!'

'It can't do any harm, Phil, to tell them that. All right, yes, I did tell Stan I was going to see mother, and that I wouldn't be home till late.'

I said: 'I trust you found your mother well?'

30

'Oh, you fool, Anthea!' Lampard groaned.

'I – I didn't actually go there,' Mrs Reydon stammered. 'At the last moment, I changed my mind.'

'Why was that, Mrs Reydon?'

'I don't know – something! Anyway, I didn't. I went to Bertie's instead. Does it matter?'

'You are quite sure it was Bertie's?'

'Yes, I told you.'

'I ask, because no one there remembers you.'

'But they must!'

'The first account we have of you is your following your husband up Lime Walk.'

'Oh lord.' Her cheeks had paled. 'But I was at Bertie's. I was!'

I shook my head.

'Yes! They must have forgotten me, that's all.'

'Where were you, Mrs Reydon?'

'I was –!' And then she burst into tears: helplessly, hopelessly. And Lampard was off his chair again.

'Sit down, Mr Lampard.'

'I've had enough!'

'Nevertheless, I must ask you to sit down.'

'You bastards, you're going to have it, aren't you? You'll listen to Sara, but not to us. And now you're playing your games with Anthea, as though she hasn't had to go through enough . . .'

'Just a simple statement, Mr Lampard.'

'Tell them, Phil,' Mrs Reydon wailed. 'We'll have to tell them.'

'Anthea, I wanted to save you from this!'

Mrs Reydon wept on Lampard's chest.

Tanner winked at Mary. 'Let's have some more tea, love. I can see this going on all night.'

Mary went to fetch tea. I lit my pipe. Mrs Reydon continued weeping on a stone-faced Lampard.

31

'Just don't get the wrong impression – there's nothing like that between me and Anthea!'

The tea had been fetched, and Mrs Reydon persuaded to take some sips from her mug. She sat hugging herself, and staring, her cheeks still pale and raddled with tears. Lampard was sitting again. He looked warm, had pulled open his collar and tie. He gave Mary a dirty look as she scribbled on her pad. And waited.

'If you want the facts, we met eight months ago, before she and her husband moved into the Walk. That was at a party to cement a deal that Reydon Contracts had put my way. I'm in building supply. I don't have to tell you that the recession is hitting us hard. Well, Reydon's got me a long-term contract with the local borough council, and it was worth a slap-up dinner. And that's where I first met Anthea.'

'At Bertie's.'

'Right.' He paused. 'Sara told you?'

'Yes.'

'Well, you can draw your own conclusions! Perhaps it wasn't altogether his fault, though Anthea tells me she's had plenty to put up with. At first I didn't notice, or perhaps I didn't want to. Reydon had done me a favour with that contract, and Sara . . . I thought I'd got Sara straightened out! But Anthea had spotted it. She told me. I couldn't believe it, right off. So Anthea said, if I needed hard proof, we only had to provide the right opportunity.'

'Which – you did?'

'I rang Sara from the office, told her I'd be working late on a set of estimates, not to wait up. And Anthea – well, you know what she told Reydon.'

'I – I visit my mother every week,' Mrs Reydon faltered. 'I'm always late back when I visit her.'

I said to Lampard: 'Go on.'

'We met over by the Park. This would be around sixish.

32

I'd swopped my Merc for a rented Escort. First we drove up the Walk and back to see if there were lights in Anthea's house. There weren't. There were plenty in mine. So we found a space and parked across from it. And there we bloody well sat it out till we saw Sara see him out of the door.'

'Why didn't you go in?'

'I couldn't, could I? The damned fellow might not have been there, and then what a jealous fool I'd have looked. No, we waited, listened to the radio, watched a few other things going on there. And in the end it paid off. Him and her, saying good-night.'

Mrs Reydon groaned. 'She was plastered to him.'

'I must admit I was seething,' Lampard said. 'I wanted to confront them, but Anthea held me back, said we didn't want any scandal.'

'Yet you did follow him.'

'All right, I did! I had every intention of having it out with him. We were going to follow him into the house and have a private session there. So we let him go ahead, and followed up on the opposite pavement. And then, just as he turned towards his steps, this fellow came out from behind the tree.'

'Before that, you hadn't seen him?'

'No. And the Walk was deserted but for us.'

'Try to remember exactly what you saw.'

Mrs Reydon shuddered. 'He was suddenly there. It was so sudden.'

'He came out like a cat,' Lampard said. 'Big, and black. I doubt if Reydon heard a thing. Three or four strides, then he was hitting him, and Reydon screamed and went down.'

'And the man?'

'That woman shouted, and he was gone like a puff of smoke.'

'Into the mews?'

'It had to be. There was nowhere else he could have gone.'

'And you?'

'I ran over to Reydon. I think he was still breathing when I got there. If I should have left the knife in, I'm sorry. It just seemed the natural thing to do.'

'And the man – you saw no more of him?'

'No. The next thing I was having to hold back Anthea. She would have thrown herself down on Reydon, but it was useless, I couldn't let her. Then the woman who'd shouted came out of her house and told us she'd rung 999. Then other people came, and the police car. And you.'

'It just wasn't true!' Mrs Reydon whimpered. 'I couldn't believe what was happening. The man. And Stan lying there. It was like a bad dream.'

I said: 'Would you know if your husband had made any enemies?'

'No. What enemies should he have made?'

'Say, in the line of his business?'

'No. No. Stan got on with everyone. That's why he was so successful.'

Lampard said grudgingly: 'You had to like him, even though you thought he might be doing you down. He was good, could swing a deal. He earned the commission I was paying him.'

'No big interests he might have offended?'

'Shouldn't have thought so,' Lampard said.

'I was his secretary before I married him,' Mrs Reydon said. 'And there was nothing like that. Nothing.'

'And nothing further you can add – either of you?'

Lampard paused, then shook his head.

Mrs Reydon said: 'It happened the way Phil told it. There's nothing I can add to that.'

'Neither of you caught a glimpse of the man's face?'

'Oh no!'

'We were across the street from him,' Lampard said. 'We only saw him from behind. And it was all over in seconds.'

'His clothes. His hair?'

'A black coat. I think. And his hair . . . it wasn't dark.'

'Fair hair?'

'I couldn't swear to that, but it wasn't dark. That's all I can say.'

'And a guess at his age?'

Lampard shrugged. 'Between thirty and fifty is all I can tell you. The way he moved, he could have been younger. But if you want a guess, I'd say forty.'

'Forty.'

'At a guess.'

Mrs. Reydon said nothing.

'Very well, then.' I glanced at Tanner, who merely shook his head. I said: 'I'm afraid we must detain you a little longer, while your statements are being prepared.'

Lampard's beard came up. 'And then?'

'When you have signed them, you will be free to go.'

'You mean – no more of this nonsense of Sara's?'

'For the moment, that will be all.'

They were escorted out. I drank some cold tea. Tanner lit a weary cheroot. He toyed a moment with the match, then broke it and dropped it into his ashtray. He said:

'In this business we see it all! So we're back with the mugger, are we, sir?'

I shook my head. 'I wouldn't bank on it. Not from the way it's being told.'

'I was believing that geezer,' Tanner said. 'I didn't want to, but I was. Once he was telling a straight story. And the lady too. I reckon she's kosher.'

'Probably kosher.'

35

Tanner breathed smoke. 'So tomorrow we chase that knife,' he said. 'Maybe and maybe not. A long shot. But we'll chase it.'

'Any advance on the description will help.'

'Now he's got fair hair,' Tanner said. 'Maybe forty, six feet, wears a black coat when he's on the job. Could be me, sir.'

'It wasn't, was it?'

'Naow! I was home with the wife and kids. But talking of that, I'd better rustle up some transport, or your wife will be having my guts for garters.'

Just a single patrol car remained in Lime Walk, parked across from the pale spot on the pavement. The light was on in our bedroom. I found Gabrielle, still dressed, asleep on the bed, clutching my pyjamas. She woke with a start.

'Oh – it's you!' She rubbed her eyes fiercely. 'What time is it?'

I told her. Then she jumped up suddenly, and grabbed me. She said:

'Tell me, George – tell me! What happened out there wasn't real, was it?'

3

Had it been real?

I slept late, having rung the Yard the night before; and it was the clamour of the phone in the hall that woke me from my slumber. I didn't hurry myself. Gabrielle still slept. I went to the window and raised the blind. Outside, a thin sunlight warmed a perfectly normal-looking Lime Walk. The patrol car had gone. Mrs Cartwright had long since taken in her milk. A woman I recognized was setting out for the shops with a cooing youngster in a pram. So very normal! And yet . . .

From our window, the exact spot wasn't visible.

'Gently here.'

'Hullo, you old scoundrel! They tell me you're taking in washing now.'

It was Paget, my colleague at the Yard. But somehow I wasn't in the mood for his banter.

'What's come in?'

'You're asking me – you, with bodies cluttering your doorstep? It was a joke at conference this morning. Even the AC managed a smile.'

I said: 'So what? The locals are handling it.'

'Not any more they aren't, old cock. Since you were so close to being in at the death, the AC thinks you should carry on. Have you seen the papers?'

'No.'

'Your stiff made the stop press in two of them. But no names, not to worry. They're treating it as just another mugging.'

'Have the locals been advised?'

'They were ringing bells. That Tanner is a fan, or didn't you know?'

Perhaps I'd been expecting it, but I didn't want it: I hung the phone up with a bang. It came too close! Almost at our door, and involving people we knew, neighbours. Last night I'd had to handle a couple of them – three, counting Mrs Lampard – and there might be more to come. Also, there was Gabrielle . . .

I grabbed the phone again and rang Tanner. 'Anything fresh since last night?'

'Don't think so, sir.' He sounded jaded, had probably only just got in himself. 'Patrols picked up a likely customer, and we've done him for going equipped. But that's all. Except, first thing, I had men out enquiring about the knife.'

'Has anyone been round to Reydon's office?'

'Not yet.'

'Leave it. I'll call in myself.'

'Right you are, sir. I don't mind telling you, I was bucked to hear they were letting us keep you.'

I grunted. 'Have the press been after you?'

'Yes, sir. But nothing I couldn't handle.'

Gabrielle appeared as I was pouring our tea. Her eyes told me she had heard those two conversations. She took her cup silently and sat down on a chair by the kitchen table. I sat down by her. She drank, then gave a rueful little grimace.

'At least, I shall have you here at home!'

I said: 'You don't have to stay.'

'Ha?'

38

'There's always Heatherings. And you will be alone here for most of the time.'

She stared, then shook her head firmly. 'No, my dear.'

'It might be best.'

'You say? Then who shall shop and get meals for you, and protect you from blondes like the good Mrs Lampard?' She drank. 'I stay,' she said. 'I am not to be driven from this place. I have friends here. I have acquaintance. I shall not care about a body on the pavement. I am your wife, and shall I not be here, each time you put your key in the door?'

I bowed my head.

'It is settled, then?'

I went for a quick shower and a shave. At the door, Gabrielle gave me a fervid hug, then went in and closed the door quickly.

The sun, or some other agency, had reduced the pale spot to a mere ghost, and I deliberately kept to the pavement on that side as I set out down Lime Walk. I paused for a moment beside the tree, below which yellow leaves had collected. But Tanner's men had been there before me, and leaves lying over tarmac offer few clues. A couple of leaves lay on the red Porsche, a few on the steps that Reydon hadn't reached. The house looked very empty. Mrs Reydon, I knew, had been dropped at her mother's. I passed on. The sun was almost indecent after the grey chill of the day before, somehow mocking, as though the sullen weather had lasted only until . . .

I counted the numbers on the sunny terraces until I located Lampard's house. It was one of those in the turn where the Walk came in from the direction of the Church Street. Thus it faced up the Walk. I had a memory of a maroon Mercedes parked there. But not now. And if there had been a rented Escort, it no longer remained to disgrace our yuppie backwater. In my mind's eye I could see where they had probably parked it, where another surviving tree would cast a shadow, in view of the house, but obscure: it fitted. From there, they had watched Reydon set forth on his last walk . . .

I hastened out into the Church Street, people, traffic, another scene. About half-way along was a small, modern office block which I had seen before, without really noticing. Beside swing doors a brass plate was inscribed: Reydon Contracts. I pushed through them, and entered a reception area smelling faintly of polish and tobacco smoke. The reception was unmanned. Behind a glass screen I could see office staff standing around, discussing together. I rang a bell on the counter; reluctantly, a girl detached herself and came through.

'I'm sorry, but if you could come back tomorrow . . .'

'Police.'

'Oh, yes . . . of course.'

'Is there someone in charge here?'

'You'll want Mr Hicks. He's upstairs, in his office.'

She led me up a flight of stairs to a furnished hall on the first floor, and knocked on a door from behind which I could hear voices.

'What do you want?'

'It's the police, Mr Hicks.'

I was shown into a bleak but businesslike office. A corpulent man of about fifty rose from behind a spacious metal desk, and his companion, a younger man, hastily stubbed out a cigarette. Almost automatically, the corpulent man thrust out his hand.

'I'm Hicks, Mr Reydon's manager, and this is my assistant, Jonesy! I'm afraid we're all at sixes and sevens here, but they did ring me to expect you . . . Janet, fetch some coffee, and tell them not to put through any calls.'

He had a fruity voice with a trace of cockney, jowls, a bald patch, and lively brown eyes. His assistant was a serious-faced man with a small moustache and a blotchy complexion.

'Have you caught the bloke yet?'

I shook my head.

'Well, the sooner he's put away the better! You can't walk the streets these days. It's been a shock to us here, I can tell you.'

'When did you learn the news?'

'This morning. The lady rang when I was in my bath. Carry on as usual was what she said – I ask you! As yet, we don't know whether we're coming or going. Do you think she'll take over?'

'Is she capable of it?'

'I dunno, but it wouldn't surprise me. She was Stanley's right hand before he married her, and she strikes you as having her head screwed on.'

'How did she sound on the phone?'

'A bit het up. But she was with it.'

'She actually saw what happened.'

Hicks stared. 'Well you'd never have known it, just talking to her on the phone.'

Janet came back with a tray, and was dismissed. We took seats round the desk, and drank coffee. The window of the office looked directly on to the Church Street and the buzz and rumble of traffic sounded persistently in the background. Hicks was frowning, Jonesy looking worried. Hicks said:

'There's nothing rum about this, is there? I mean, it's happening all the time. A bloke was mugged out here last month.'

I said: 'Exactly what business do you carry on here?'

'How do you mean – what business?'

I said: 'I understand that you work on a commission basis. Perhaps you would be kind enough to explain that.'

'Ah,' Hicks said. 'Yes. Well, it's the law of supply and demand, isn't it? You've got people who want building done on the one side, and contractors and builder's suppliers on the other.'

'And you act as brokers?'

'You could say that. We keep the contractors and suppliers on our books. Then we snout out the projects that are coming along, and match the one lot with the other. So everyone's happy. It pays both sides. The customer gets the best job, and completed on time. The contractors and suppliers get some business they'd never have known about, but for us.'

'And it all works smoothly?'

'Give or take.'

'Never, for example, a conflict of interest?'

'Not if we can help it. We balance it out. If a client loses this one, he wins the next.'

'Have you had clients go broke?'

'Not because of us. I dare say the recession has caught one or two. But then, we've been a lifeline for some of the others, you can ask around. We earn our cut.'

'I believe a Mr Lampard was a satisfied client.'

Hicks and his assistant exchanged a quick look.

'You'll have been doing your homework!' Hicks said. 'But the answer is yes. We did give him a leg-up.'

'Wasn't there a party to celebrate the contract?'

'A bit of a knees-up in Bertie's.'

'You were there?'

'Me and the missus. But we didn't see anything out of the way.' Hicks drank some coffee. 'You have to ask these things. Me, I don't think there was anything in it. Or not much. Just office gossip. I can't think it had to do with what happened last night.'

'Would you know if there had been other such occasions?'

'Well, Stanley . . . there you are! The girls thought he was a hunk.'

'Recently?'

'Not that I know of.' He glanced at Jonesy, who shook his head.

I, too, drank coffee. I said: 'Getting back to the business! Is it possible that Mr Reydon had some rivals?'

'Nobody's throat he cut,' Hicks said. 'I dare say there are some who won't be shedding any tears.'

'No enemies?'

'None I would call that.'

'Then how about closer to home?'

'How do you mean?' Hicks looked wary.

'I mean members of his staff who he may have offended.'

Hicks was about to shake his head, but then his eyes went suddenly still. He stared at Jonesy, Jonesy stared back, and Hicks extended a pudgy, accusatory finger.

'That bastard Salmon. Him!'

'Yes, Mr Hicks. Him!'

'And I wouldn't put it past him, a trick like that.'

'No, Mr Hicks. He did threaten me.'

'He threatened you?'

'Yes, he did. When he heard Mr Reydon had given me his job. He said if he ever found out I'd shopped him, he'd do for me on some dark night.'

'He said he'd do for you?'

'Yes, Mr Hicks.'

Hicks turned to me. 'You asked,' he said. 'And there's your answer. We had a wrong'un here called Jack Salmon, who Stanley sacked for milking the till.'

I said: 'When was this?'

'Six weeks, a couple of months ago. He was doing Jonesy's job, but I never liked the surly bastard. Then we copped him in the act, and Stanley fired him. And you heard what Jonesy has just told us.'

43

'Can you describe him?'

'You bet. A beefy sod, going six foot.'

'Colouring?'

'Reddish chops, fair hair and grey eyes.'

'Age?'

'Mid-forties.'

'Do we have his address?'

'Look in the files, Jonesy,' Hicks said. 'I seem to remember him living in Bloemfontein Road, but I can't recollect the exact number.'

Jonesy delved in a filing cabinet drawer and came up with a crumpled sheet. Hicks scanned it frowningly. 'Here we are! Number 178, Bloemfontein Road. I see he was with us for six years, and my assistant for two of them. He did his job, I'll give him that, but I wasn't sorry to see the back of him. Do you think he's the one?'

I shrugged and took the sheet. Salmon had been a builder's foreman before he joined Reydon's. Married, two children, car allowance, a previous address in Earls Court. And two red lines across the bottom of his sheet, along with the inscription: Dismissed for dishonesty. I said:

'Have you heard of him since?'

'No. But I've seen him around once or twice.'

'Would he have found a fresh job?'

'I shouldn't think it likely. He sure as hell didn't get a reference from us.'

Certainly, he sounded a useful prospect: sacked from what was probably a well-paid job, without hope of fresh employment, nursing his resentment as the cash got shorter. I said:

'If I may, I'll keep this sheet. Have there been any other disgruntled employees?'

Hicks thought about it, looked at Jonesy. Jonesy said:

'There was only Henry, sir.'

'Henry! He'd never have done it.'

'No. But he was sacked, sir.'

Hicks frowned, and stared for a moment. 'I wasn't going to mention Henry,' he said. 'It was rather a sad case, and I'm damned sure that Henry would never kill anyone.' He drank some cold coffee. 'Henry Saxby,' he said. 'Everyone here was sorry for him. I guess he caught Stanley in the wrong mood, or surely Stanley would never have sacked him.'

'He was employed here?'

'Our chief clerk. A fellow who wouldn't say boo to a goose. He had a sick wife. She went into hospital. Stanley cracked down on him taking time off to visit her. But Henry went all the same. And in the end, Stanley sacked him.'

'And the wife?'

'The wife died.'

'When was this?' I said.

'August. We sent flowers. I think all the staff here contributed.'

'And since then?'

Hicks shook his head. 'At Henry's age, you don't stand a chance. It's tragic. You see him hanging about. They didn't have children, it was just him and her. Come to that, I suppose now I could re-employ him, as long as the widow has no objection.'

'All the same, I think I'd better have his description.'

Reluctantly Hicks complied. Henry Saxby, fifty-two, around five foot ten, lean build, greying, resident at 22 Randall Road, jobless and widower since mid-August.

'Do you have his sheet?'

I took that too. Then, as I was leaving, the telephone rang. Hicks handed it to me. It was Tanner. His men had located the source of the knife.

'Wilf Liddle, sir. He's on his way now. He runs an Army

and Navy off Hammersmith Broadway. He recognized the knife straight away because of that bit of horn missing from the handle.'

'When was it bought?'

'That's the cream of it. He sold it last thing yesterday afternoon.'

'And he can describe the customer?'

'Six foot, black coat, and may have been fair. But he was wearing a hat.'

I hadn't hurried on my way to the police station: I was still contemplating that last sorry prospect Hicks had given me. Henry Saxby, the mild-mannered clerk, whom tragedy had struck twice in those sultry August days. A man who would never kill anyone, Hicks had said, a gentle man, a victim. But, in my long experience of such affairs, I had seen men like Saxby pushed over the edge. His wife had died, when? While he was still being kept apart from her? It fitted too well with the killing we'd heard described, the sudden, ruthless plunge of the knife: the revenge of a man driven beyond bearing. It fitted the clerk better than the bully-boy Salmon.

'Sir, I was thinking of an identity parade for our pal Lampard. At least it would keep the screw on.'

'For Lampard?'

'He's still our best customer.'

I shook my head. 'Lampard can wait.'

'I don't know, sir,' Tanner said. 'As I see it he's still got plenty going for him. He could just as well have been behind that tree as sitting it out in the car with the lady. All Mrs Cartwright sees is his back, and him disappearing into the alley. Then she slams her door, so there's no one to say he didn't come back again to act the innocent.'

'That would involve Mrs Reydon.'

'Yes, sir. And I wouldn't say no to that. Between you and

me she's a bit of a cool customer, and she had plenty to play for there.'

'You mean, the business?'

Tanner nodded.

I thought about it, then shook my head. 'Remember I was there within minutes of it happening. I doubt if she could have acted that part. Improvisation would have been necessary. Mrs Cartwright's presence was unforeseen.'

'Wouldn't have needed much, sir, just a touch here and there. And Lampard is the only lead we have, it won't do any harm to keep him sweating.'

'No.' I produced the two personnel dockets. 'Because now we do have other leads. So we'll leave Lampard on the back burner, and issue pick-ups on these two men.'

I brought Tanner up to date. He listened cautiously at first. Then, when I mentioned Salmon's name, a gleam came into his eye.

'Jack Salmon, sir?'

'Jack Dennis Salmon.'

'We've had him in here twice for being d. and d.'

'So you know him?'

'I know him, sir. And so do the men who brought him in. He gave one of them a black eye and knee'd the other one where he shouldn't. I haven't heard of him carrying a blade before, but it wouldn't surprise me to learn he did.'

'Six feet, with fair hair.'

'Absolutely right, sir – he'll fit the bill to a t. And Reydon sacked him for robbing the till?'

I nodded.

'Yes,' Tanner said. 'I like it. I like it.'

'Then there's this other fellow.'

I introduced him to Saxby, but I felt I hadn't got all his attention. Saxby, after all, was under size, had only grey hair, and no police record. Salmon was the hot one. Tanner was listening, but he was itching to pick up the phone.

47

'Perhaps later on, sir . . .'

'I want Saxby picked up.'

'Yes sir, of course, we'll have him too. But he doesn't sound so much of a spec, and I've met Salmon, I know his form.'

'And if he has an alibi?'

'Yes, of course, you're right, sir. Only this Saxby sounds a bit of a wet. Still, we'll have him. As you say, he has motive. We'd better hear what he's got to say.'

He lifted the phone: there was a tap on the door.

'Sir,' a DC said. 'We've brought Mr Liddle.'

'Ask him to wait,' Tanner said, and went on giving instructions to the phone.

'This here is another one of them, see? It's got my price-sticker on the handle. 'Course, I knew it was the same knife as soon as your busy shoved it on the counter. They're a lot I bought up east. Nothing comic about them, was there?'

An anxious, elderly little cockney with lined features and sharp blue eyes. He'd brought a matching knife in a brown paper bag, and now laid it beside the other on Tanner's desk. Two cheap, 'hunting'-style knives, their horn handles almost certainly plastic. The example Liddle had brought wore a sheath of a coarse leather, that smelled.

'This knife was defective when you sold it?'

'That's right, squire.' Liddle gave me a knowing wink. 'I wouldn't say any of them were right down perfect, and that one didn't have a sheath, neither. So I put it in the odds and sods box – you'd be surprised what you can sell that way! And this geezer came up when I was closing. I let him have it for a nicker.'

'Would you recognize him again?'

'Could do. I wouldn't know.'

'Tell me about him.'

'Well, he came in when I was closing, didn't he?'

'So?'

'I was humping the gear in. I'd let Sid and Mave go early. And it was blinking freezing out there, I just wanted to get done and go home. So this geezer sidles up to the odds and sods box just as I'm about to hump it in, grabs the knife out and asks me what I'll take for it. I tell him a nicker, he hoists it out, and that's the last I see of him.'

'A tall man?'

'About your clip, squire.'

'Wearing a black coat?'

'Coat, hat and muffler. Looked a bit seedy, you could have took him for a dosser. But I dunno. He didn't speak like one.'

'His appearance may have been misleading.'

'If you say so. He'd got this hat jammed over his ears. Then there was the muffler, and his coat collar turned up, I dunno. I only saw him for a minute.'

'What struck you about his face?'

'Well – bleeding nothing!'

'He was clean-shaven?'

Liddle shook his head. 'All this was out in the street, and me wanting to get shut of him and go home. There was only the light showing from my window, I never did get a decent look at him. Just him grabbing the knife from the box and feeling for a nicker, and shoving off.'

'But you noticed his hair.'

'I think he was fair.'

'You think?'

'That's just an impression!'

'Could it have been grey?'

'I can't swear to it, squire, and that's the honest truth. I am doing my best.'

'And . . . his age?'

49

'If you want me to guess, I'd say he was somewhere close to fifty.'

'Anything else about him?'

'Stone me,' Liddle said. 'Before I came here, I wouldn't have said I knew as much.'

He was dismissed to write his statement, taking his spare knife and paper bag with him. Were we any further forward? I lit my pipe, and Tanner one of his cheroots. Tanner said:

'We could still have that line-up, see how Lampard stands up to that.' But he didn't sound hopeful. I said:

'Perhaps we should keep the line-up for Salmon.'

Tanner drew smoke. 'Whichever it is, we're dealing with a tricky bastard! He got himself up when he bought that knife, then left it till the bloke was closing his shop. Ten to one Liddle can't pick him out, and he's the only card we've got.'

'He said you could have taken him for a dosser.'

'That's what I mean, sir. He fixed himself up like a tramp.'

'Either that, or we're dealing with an unknown quantity.'

Tanner stared. 'I can't really believe that, sir.'

I puffed a few times. 'It's an outside chance. We still have to look at Salmon and Saxby. But if neither one of them adds up, we may have to cast our net wider.'

Tanner kept staring. 'I don't buy it, sir. The way it was done, it wasn't a mugging. Someone was out to get Reydon, and it had to be someone with good reason.'

'A revenge killing. Or something else.'

'But . . . what could that something else be?'

I shrugged. 'We're looking at a man engaged in an unusual line of business. Some toes he must have trodden on, perhaps those of powerful interests. And his death is a crime bearing the marks of planning. It's an outside chance, but we can't ignore it.'

50

Tanner smoked hard. 'You mean – someone paid chummie?'

I nodded. 'That's what it may imply.'

'Then . . . we're after a pro?'

'It's not impossible. And an interest that found Reydon and his business an obstacle.'

Tanner sat frowning at the knife on his desk, from which the traces of blood had been removed. Then he flicked his cheroot impatiently.

'Sorry, sir, but I can't buy that! Not with a bloke like Salmon tied up in it, and Mrs Lampard and all.'

'Just an outside bet,' I said.

'I'll keep my money on Salmon, sir. With a side bet on pal Lampard. I'm not giving him a clear run yet.'

'Did you check his account of renting an Escort?'

'Yes, sir. All kosher there. And I took his dabs, which he didn't think much of, and they were all we could find on the knife.'

'A pity about that.'

'A great pity. But it could be his grief before we're through.'

'So now,' I said, 'we wait for Salmon. And Saxby.'

'Yes, sir.' And the gleam was back in Tanner's eye.

4

But it proved less than a straightforward business to locate the two ex-employees of Reydon Contracts.

At Bloemfontein Road, the patrolmen on the errand encountered only Salmon's less-than-sociable wife. No, Jackie wasn't in, and likely wouldn't be back all day. Where was he? They'd better bloody look for him, hadn't they, and perhaps they could tell her when they found him.

In Randall Road, there was just a locked door and a note in a milk bottle reading: Not Today. A neighbour said she hadn't seen Saxby since yesterday, and added that he kept most unusual hours.

'Do you think Salmon has skipped, sir?'

It wasn't improbable. 'Better put out an alert.'

'If he's skipped, then he's sussed that we're on to him.'

But my thoughts were rather with the lonely former clerk.

I said: 'Can we rustle up a search warrant for Saxby's?'

'Saxby's, sir?' Tanner's eyes were alert.

'If he didn't come home, he's been missing too long. And if he did – well, we want to know that.'

'Oh lor'!' Tanner said. 'I see what you mean, sir. I'll get that warrant right away.'

I left it to be sent after me, and set out on foot into the busy streets. The early sun had faded now, and a chill mist was seeping up from the river. Shops, stores were decorated for Christmas, putting a sparkle into the gloom: already a Christmas tree was being erected, and illuminations strung from lamp-posts.

I left the glitter, and entered drab streets where rusted cars lined the pavements. Such a one was Randall Road, though it did own the distinction of a few leafless plane trees. I found 22 in a red-brick terrace. The milk bottle and note stood as reported. Curtains were drawn, windows looked grimy, dead leaves and a crisp packet lay on the step. I rapped with the knocker: the sound echoed hollowly. Nothing stirred at 22.

'It's no good, dearie, he isn't in there.'

A woman had come to the door of 24. Plump, round-faced, with curious dark eyes, she had a brush and dustpan in her hands.

'The police were here earlier, dearie, but they didn't have any luck either. I don't know where the beggar has got to. What's he done – robbed a bank?'

I introduced myself. The lady gazed at me.

'Gordon Bennet – you're slumming, ain't you? So what's it about?'

'We wish to talk to Mr Saxby.'

'But a bloke like you. What's he done?'

Her name was Mrs Dawson, she told me, and she had lived next door for twenty years. For most of that time she had known the Saxbys, who she thought had moved there from Walham Green way.

'I knew her better than I knew him. She was a real nice woman, Ada Saxby. We used to have a drink at The Marquis together, and a bit of a sing-song, you know.'

'He was fond of his wife?'

'Lived for her, didn't he? Nothing was too good for Ada. They was thinking of buying a place in Somerleyton Gardens. Then she went down with this funny disease.'

'Did he take it badly?'

'What? Never been the same man again, has he? Went to pieces he did. Lost his job. It's a blinking shame what it did to him. He was always a quiet bloke, of course, you didn't often see him down at the pub, but he was all right. I kind of liked him. He was a cut above some of the sods around here.'

'I believe his life recently has been irregular.'

She stared as though she didn't quite understand. 'He ain't running after women, if that's what you mean! I reckon a good woman might do him some good.'

'Is he often out at night?'

'Ah, now I'm with you. Yes, you can't tell what he gets up to. Sometimes he hangs around the house, and another time it's like now. And he doesn't care, you know? He doesn't look after himself like he used to. Once he was a real smart bloke, but these days you could take him for a beggar.'

'When was the last time you saw him?'

'Ah.' At once Mrs Dawson's eyes were wary. 'Now you're talking like a copper. So what's the poor bloke supposed to have done?'

I said: 'He may be able to help us with some enquiries we are making.'

'Yes, but what sort of enquiries? We don't see toffs like you when it's shop-lifting.'

I told her. Her eyes rounded. She stepped back a pace, staring at me. Then she shook her head decidedly.

'You have to be barking up the wrong tree, dearie!'

'At the moment, we are accusing Mr Saxby of nothing.'

'And you better hadn't, because he'd never have done it. I can think of one or two round here who might have, but not him, not poor old Henry.'

I said: 'Shall I say we are concerned about him?'

'You can say what you like, can't you?'

'That he has come to no harm.'

54

'What bleeding harm?'

I turned my eyes to the house.

'Oh, Gawd!'

I said: 'So when did you last see him?'

She was silent for a moment, gazing at the house. Then she muttered:

'Bloody lunch time, wasn't it? I saw him go past here, going towards the Church Street.'

'Do you remember what he was wearing?'

'His coat and titfer.'

'Can you remember the colour of his coat?'

'I dunno. Brown, wasn't it? It's the old coat he always wears.'

'Not grey. Or black?'

'No! His old brown coat with the frayed sleeves. And his old titfer jammed on his bonce. You'd have thought he came from cardboard city.'

'Was he wearing a scarf?'

'Couldn't see that, could I, not him with his collar turned up.'

'Can you estimate the time?'

'Round two I should think. *Neighbours* was over, I can tell you that.'

'And you haven't seen him since?'

She shook her head. 'I'd have heard him if he was back there, them walls are like paper. He couldn't be there and me not know it.'

'You were in all the time?'

'Ah – no. I sometimes give a hand at The Marquis.'

'Till when was that?'

'Be midnight, wouldn't it? After we'd finished washing up the glasses.'

And suddenly we were both staring up at the house, and Mrs Dawson had edged a little closer to me. Other women had appeared at their doors, and I noticed a curtain twitch across the road.

A patrol car arrived with two uniform men and DI Pyatt. Pyatt had the search warrant, and one of the men a bunch of keys. I gave the door a second, perfunctory, knock, then signalled to the man to get to work. The women were out in the street now, collecting in a group at a little distance. Mrs Dawson had stood her ground, watching with rounded, frowning eyes.

Later, we would need her statement: but she certainly wasn't going to run away.

Finally the lock succumbed. We left a man outside, and went in. The house had a fusty, unaired smell, and dust was thick on the stairs and furnishings. Yet it wasn't a poverty-stricken place. The furniture, the carpets were modern, and of quality. The kitchen, though small, was fully fitted, as was the little bathroom upstairs. But every-where, signs of neglect: dust, litter, an overflowing swing-bin. Same in the small paved yard outside. In the sink, the dirty crockery of several meals past.

'He isn't up here, sir.'

'Check the yard.'

The yard contained a coal-shed and an outside loo. More lumber, but no Saxby. And no body to cut down from a convenient hook.

'He'll have gone on the loose, sir.'

'Put out an alert.'

Upstairs, the bed had not been slept in, and dregs in a teacup in the sink were dry. Since two o'clock yesterday he had been adrift in his threadbare coat, his dragged-down hat...

I prowled round the house, found bills unpaid, an empty fridge, a stinking bread-bin. On the sitting-room mantelpiece, a silver-framed photograph of a smiling woman with fading hair. Upstairs a wardrobe was full of her clothes, her jewellery, brushes, combs on the dressing-table. Her shoes. A bottle of scent. In drawers, her underwear and an odour of violets. I looked for, but didn't find, a photograph of Saxby, only some others of his wife. Had he made away with them? A calendar on the wall was still showing the month of September.

'We shall need to leave a man here.'

'That's what I was thinking, sir.'

But did Saxby ever mean to return to that house? I'd found no money there, no cheque book: just a bank sheet showing him to be in low water.

We went back into the street to find Mrs Dawson surrounded by her neighbours. She thrust forward eagerly.

'Have you found him?'

I merely shook my head. I couldn't tell whether she was disappointed or not. I left Pyatt to take her statement and took the car back to the police station.

I put Tanner in the picture, but he was less impressed than I would have supposed.

'We've had a sighting of Salmon since you went out, sir – I reckon we'll have him here any minute!'

'Where did you find him?'

'Over at Earls Court. He was coming away from a used car lot. Patrol lost him when he turned down a side-street, but we've got it covered. We must have him.'

'No sightings of Saxby?'

Tanner shook his head. 'Do you really rate him as a prospect, sir?'

'I rate him very strongly.'

'Well, I don't know, sir. He just sounds a bit of a nana to me.'

I said: 'I've just seen his house. Saxby is a man at the end of his tether. And he adds up pretty well to Liddle's description, not to mention those of the other witnesses.'

'But all the same, sir! Didn't the lady say he was often out, roaming around? So maybe he spent the night on a park bench, but I can't see him as the chummie in Lime Walk.'

I said: 'He left Randall Road at two p.m., giving him plenty of time to buy the knife from Liddle, and time to make his way to Lime Walk and commence a vigil outside Reydon's house. That vigil was perhaps longer than he expected. He may have planned to return home in the absence of Mrs Dawson. As it turned out, he was too late for that, and so he had to stay adrift and seek a different alibi. Presumably he hasn't found one, so he's still adrift. And I doubt if he's going back to Randall Road.'

Tanner wrinkled his face. 'Sounds a bit iffy, sir!'

'We still want Saxby under wraps at the earliest.'

'I give you that, sir. But the way you tell it, perhaps we ought to be looking for him in the Thames.'

Something else had happened while I was out: a minor disturbance at Bertie's Hotel. Apparently Lampard had presented himself there and demanded an audience with his lady. The lady had objected: Lampard had persisted: a lively slanging match ensued. Eventually we had been called in and the wrathful Lampard ejected. He had also been banned from the hotel.

'I'm told she was really giving it to him,' Tanner grinned. 'Now half of London knows he's a cuckold, and the other half thinks he's our man for Reydon. Which of course he still could be, sir. I haven't crossed him off the list.'

Had I crossed him off? Perhaps I had, a short while before, at Number 22: when I was looking at a silver-framed photograph, or inhaling the scent from a dressing-table drawer. Suddenly such a motive as Lampard's had seemed trivial, likely to lead only to a punch on the jaw: it had no depth. The blow that killed Reydon sprang from an injury more potent.

Pyatt returned with Mrs Dawson's statement. Tanner brooded over it for a while, frowning. He said:

'Well, he could have been the type, sir. Like he was one of these quiet blokes who sometimes get a rush. Is that how you see him?'

I nodded grudgingly.

'A bit of a Christie, sir,' Tanner said.

'He didn't kill his wife!'

'No, sir, not that. But living alone, letting things go to pot. A bloke who never made friends, just him and his wife, and when she goes he falls apart. So he blames Reydon, and who knows? If he did it, he could finish up just like Christie.'

'Perhaps that's going too far.'

'Maybe it is, sir. And maybe he's just a candidate for cardboard city.'

'We shall know better when we lay hands on him.'

Tanner frowned at the statement. 'If we ever do, sir!'

But then the matter became, for the moment, academic. There was a scuffling and angry voices out in reception. Then a tap on the door. A dishevelled Edith said:

'We've got Salmon here, sir. I'm afraid we had to use cuffs.'

'Listen, I could do you for unlawful arrest! I don't know nothing about nothing. I was minding my lawful business, wasn't I, and then these buggers strong-armed me over here.'

Six feet, powerful build, fair hair, pugnacious features and shifty blue-grey eyes. Wearing a variegated shell suit of which, however, the base colour was black.

'I was over at the Court to look at a car. There's nothing comic about that, is there? So then I went for a pint at the King Dick, and these rotten sods came in and busted me.'

Uneasy blue-grey eyes. The indignation was a front.

'So what I want to know is, what's it all about? I mean cuffing me in front of my mates, too.'

I nodded to Edith. 'Take the cuffs off.'

'Yes, I should bloody well think so!'

Reluctantly, Edith complied; Salmon stood chafing his wrists, sending quick little glances. I said:

'You are Jack Dennis Salmon, of Bloemfontein Road, Kensington?'

'Who the hell do you think I am?'

'Please take a seat, Mr Salmon.'

He slammed himself down on the chair placed for him.

'Ask Mary to bring her pad.'

No question now that Salmon was unhappy. There was a touch of panic in his stare as he watched Mary take her place and lay out her pencils.

'Look, what the bloody hell is this?'

'We just require your answers to some questions, Mr Salmon.'

'But I don't know nothing!'

'For a start, were you not recently employed by Stanley Reydon, of Reydon Contracts?'

His mouth hung open. 'But what's that got to do with it?'

'Please answer the question, Mr Salmon.'

'So bloody yes! I worked for the sod. But I still don't see what you're getting at.'

I said: 'I believe he sacked you.'

'Yes, but that's all over and done with!'

I said: 'We are enquiring into the death of Mr Reydon, and we are wondering if you can help us.'

'You – what?'

60

'For example, I would like an account of your movements last night.'

He stared as though I had struck him. 'Oh bloody hell! Has someone done him in?'

I said nothing.

'Look – you're after the wrong bloke. I never set eyes on the bastard last night.'

I said: 'We have the testament of witnesses.'

'Then they're lying. You can't tie me into a job like that.'

'They describe a man who might very well be you.'

'The bastards. Who are they? Who told you that?'

'Same build, height, colouring.'

'Just wait till I find out who the sods are!'

'Shortly, you may be asked to stand in a line-up. Have you any objection to that?'

'Yes, I have.'

'For the moment, can we get back to your movements for last night?'

His glare was ferocious, fearful: baffled. He said: 'You're having me on, aren't you?'

I shook my head.

'Yes, that's it! You're having me on to see if I'll cough. Well I won't, mate. Not me. I've had these tricks played on me before. So if that's all you've got, I'll be leaving, and don't any one of you try to stop me.'

I said: 'Stay where you are, Mr Salmon.'

'Why should I? Tell me that?'

'Because if you don't, I shall be obliged to arrest you. And you haven't yet begun to answer my questions.'

'I don't have to answer them!'

'Let's try this. At what time were you in Lime Walk last night?'

'Bloody . . . where?'

He'd been getting to his feet, but now he sat down again. Very suddenly.

61

'Who . . . says I was there?'

'Weren't you there?'

'What I want to know is who says so!'

'You couldn't have been seen there?'

'Listen, I was nowhere near the bloody place!'

'Say, at around eleven p.m.?'

'Bloody no!'

'And, of course . . . some while earlier?'

He was breathing fast. 'No. I'm telling you. I was never near Lime Walk last night.' He hesitated. 'Is that where . . . ?'

I stared and said nothing.

'Oh bloody hell!' Again, that look of fear and bafflement.

'Let's try this, then,' I said. 'When were you last in Hammersmith Broadway?'

'Never mind sodding Hammersmith Broadway!'

'You prefer not to answer?'

'No. What's that got to do with Lime Walk?'

I said: 'Reydon was stabbed. He was stabbed with a knife. That knife has been traced to a shop off the Broadway. We have a description of the man who bought it. And the description would fit you.'

'Fit me . . . !'

I kept staring. Now there was horror in those eyes. Salmon gazed at me, gazed at Tanner, at Mary's hesitating pencil.

'Well?'

'Fit me . . . yes! I'm being fitted all right, aren't I? You're going to have me, I can see that, though I'm as innocent as that cow there.'

'You deny buying the knife?'

'I was never down the Broadway. I was never in bloody Lime Walk. I never bought a knife. And I never cut sodding Stan Reydon. Are you getting it down?'

'A complete denial . . . ?'

'Just shove it. Shove it where the monkey kept his nuts.'

'Then, where were you last night, Salmon?'

'Minding my own business – now you mind yours!'

Slowly, I shook my head. 'I'm afraid you will have to do better than that. If you want us to accept your innocence, we shall have to know where you were last night.'

'I was minding my business!'

'No.'

He breathed yet faster. 'All bloody right, then! I was home with the wife, watching the telly.'

'Which programmes?'

'I can't tell you! It was her who had it on, I was reading my paper.'

'For the whole of the evening?'

'I was dozing, wasn't I? I saw News at Ten, I remember that. Next thing she was waking me up with the cocoa, and it was nearly twelve. We went to bed.'

'Have you anyone to confirm that?'

'Well, the wife can, can't she?'

'I think you know the answer to that, Salmon.'

'So bloody prove different. Bloody prove it!'

'We shall certainly try.' I glanced at Tanner, who nodded. He said:

'We've still got Liddle here, sir. When I got the green light on chummie I asked him to hang on.'

'Here!' Salmon said. 'Who's this Liddle? I don't know any sodding Liddle.'

I said: 'What we have to decide now, Salmon, is whether Mr Liddle knows you.'

'But –!'

'You still have objections to standing in a line-up?'

'Oh, you bastards!' Salmon said. 'You're going to sew me up somehow, aren't you, and just because I've been in here before.'

63

'If you were at home as you say, you have nothing to worry about.'

He tried to jump up: Edith helped him to sit again. He gasped:

'I want my phone call. I've a bloody right to one!'

I stared into his wild eyes, then slowly pushed the phone towards him. He fumbled with it, stabbed at the buttons, hung up and stabbed them again. He had an agonized wait, and then:

'Donna –? No, listen Donna – just bloody listen! The filth have got me, I'm down at the station – some bugger stuck a knife into bloody Reydon! No – never mind that! You know where I was last night, don't you? That's right . . . yes . . . yes. So you tell them when they come asking, OK?'

He hung up promptly, and shoved the phone back to me. Our eyes met. He jerked his away. I signalled to Edith, who touched Salmon's shoulder: Salmon rose, allowed Edith to marshal him out. Mary took her notes and followed.

'Well, well,' Tanner said. 'Well, well. Do you want the pleasure of talking to Donna, sir?'

I shook my head. 'But get a man round there promptly. And brief him about what he should be hearing.'

'I'd say it was laid on ready,' Tanner said. 'Chummie only had to switch her on. I can see it all now, him dozing by the stove, the paper slipping out of his innocent hand. What a pity we've got Liddle. Would you say we've struck lucky, sir?'

I filled my pipe. Salmon smelled of something, but of what I still wasn't certain. Tanner went happily about making his arrangements. I rang Gabrielle to say I wouldn't be back for lunch.

'I saw this, sir, hanging in the hall. She nearly had my eyes out, but I thought I'd better bring it.'

64

DC Cresswell, supported by DC Thurloe, had been Tanner's choice for Bloemfontein Road. Cresswell was carrying a dark grey coat with a black corduroy trim and black buttons.

'I spotted it at once, sir. She didn't want us inside, but I said we couldn't talk our business in the street. And there it was, sir, hanging on the hall-stand. Though she swore blind he hadn't worn it since Sunday.'

'A pity,' Tanner said. 'A pity. But I can't rig them all out in coats. Still, it's as well to know he had one. Forensic might like a look at it too.'

But there were no apparent bloodstains on that rather too spruce and stylish overcoat. Tanner laid it aside.

'Was the lady co-operative?'

Cresswell made a face. 'Wouldn't exactly say that, sir! But she'd got her story off pat. She couldn't wait to tell it to us.'

'A nice quiet evening with the telly?'

'She'd even got the programmes off, sir. From the six o'clock news till the late film. She reeled it off like the *Radio Times*.'

'And hubby's newspaper?'

'The *Standard*, sir. She had it lying on his chair.'

'And him snoozing in his slippers?'

'They was there too. Says she had to wake him a couple of times, on account of him snoring.'

Tanner sighed. 'And they really think we'll swallow it! But never mind, Cresswell, take it on the chin. And now you're back, we can run the line-up. Liddle has never clapped eyes on you, has he?'

For lack of space, the line-up was conducted in a freezing courtyard at the rear of the police station. There, a reasonable sample of male candidates had already been assembled. Some were slightly below the prescribed height, and some had less than fair hair, while the sly Tanner, with

Lampard in mind, had included a bored-looking gentleman in city clobber. Cresswell added his six feet to these. Then Edith brought out the sweating Salmon.

'Right,' Tanner said. 'You know the drill, Salmon?'

'How the hell should I know the rotten drill!'

'You can stand in any spot in the line, sonny. Wherever you think you won't be noticed.'

'But why bloody should I? You've talked to Donna, haven't you?'

'Never mind Donna,' Tanner said. 'Just do what you're told, like a good little boy, and we'll all get in out of the cold.'

He gave Salmon a nudge: finally, Salmon just added himself to the end of the line, where he stood, still sweating, and gazing helplessly at the police station roof.

'Fetch Liddle.'

The little shopkeeper was looking almost as apprehensive as Salmon. He received his instructions, and set out uncertainly along the line of shivering prospects. He paused at the city gent, who loftily ignored him, and again at Cresswell, who looked straight through him; at last he came to the sweating Salmon, hesitated, paused, then turned away. I could almost hear Tanner holding his breath. Slowly, Liddle continued down the back of the line-up. Then, without having touched anyone, he returned uncertainly to Tanner.

'That geezer on the end – is he the one?'

'You're telling me,' Tanner said.

'It could've been him, I don't know. I'd p'raps know better if he said something.'

Tanner glanced at me. I shrugged. 'What do you want him to say?' Tanner asked.

'Well . . . any blinking thing! Like how much the doggie is in the window.'

66

After a pause, Tanner beckoned to Salmon, who, after another pause, slouched across to us. Tanner said:

'Just repeat after me. How much is that doggie in the window?'

'I do – what?'

'Just repeat what I said.'

'Like hell I will!' Salmon glared at him. 'This is some bloody trap, isn't it? One way or the other you're out to get me.'

'You don't want to say it?'

'Get stuffed!'

'Right,' Tanner said. 'Take him back inside, Edith.' Then he looked at the little shopkeeper, who had stood by listening with a screwed-up face. 'Well?'

'It ain't him, squire.'

'It – isn't?'

Liddle shook his head. 'Got a husky voice, this other one, like it had been out in the rain all night.'

'You could swear to that?' I said.

'Finger wet and finger dry.'

'I don't have to remind you how much rests on it.'

'That's why I'm telling you, squire. It ain't him.'

We went back into the office. Tanner slumped down and lit a cheroot. He said:

'Sod it and double sod it. I'm sorry, sir. But what do we do now?'

I said: 'Better hand Salmon his Sunday coat.'

'And I was so effing certain,' Tanner said. 'I mean, Donna and all. And the way he was acting. I could have sworn we were on to pay-dirt.'

'Perhaps on to something,' I said. 'But not this. It might be as well to check his alibi further.'

'You mean, just a chance that Liddle is wrong?'

I shook my head and felt for my pipe.

The telephone rang.

'Someone wants you, sir.'

I took the phone. 'Gently here.' For a moment I could hear only hoarse breathing and a faint background of passing traffic. Then:

'You're on to Saxby, aren't you?'

'Who is this speaking?'

Just the breathing; then:

'He's the man you want.' And the phone was hung up. Two sentences: in a voice that had been out in the rain.

5

Two sentences, in a voice . . . could it possibly have been Saxby himself? At least of one thing I felt chillingly certain: I had just been talking to the killer himself, the man who had brutally stabbed Stanley Reydon. A local call: it could well have come from one of the boxes in the Church Street, from which now the caller would be hastening away to lose himself among the Christmas shoppers.

Or – would he? If it had been Saxby, did he really want to avoid being arrested? Hadn't the crime itself been a desperate plea to be helped out of his intolerable loneliness? It had happened before. In such situations, men had killed to escape their hopeless alienation, to be reunited, even at this level, with humanity that seemed to have cast them off utterly. I hung up. I said:

'Send a patrol to comb the Church Street. Our man may be there, hanging about a phone box.'

'You mean – that was him?'

'I think it likely. And I think he may want to come in from the cold.'

'Saxby . . . ?'

I nodded. 'That's my guess. Saxby come to the end of the line.'

'Well . . . stone the crows!'

Tanner hastened to comply, ordered two patrols to converge on the Church Street. Shortly Saxby, if he were there, would see one or other of the cars drifting towards him. Would he panic? He knew the back streets of Kensington. Reydon's killer had vanished from the scene in minutes. It might be that not yet was he ready to submit, or that his heart might fail at the sight of his hunters.

Perhaps, it would be several days later when the wretched ex-clerk crept into reception, fearful, afraid of being manhandled. Unless the Thames had claimed him first.

Tanner said: 'I still can't quite buy it, sir! For me, this charlie wouldn't have had the bottle. I can see how he wouldn't have loved Reydon, but that's a long way from laying for him with a knife.'

I said: 'And if the same thing had happened to you?'

Tanner wriggled his shoulders. 'I'm me, sir, and he's him. I might have got round to giving Reydon a bashing, but that's as far as it would have gone.'

'Perhaps Saxby wasn't capable of giving Reydon a bashing.'

'No, sir. But then, was he up to using a knife? All we hear of him is he's a bit of a willy, nothing violent about him at all.'

'He'd had time to remember.'

'I dare say, sir.' But still Tanner didn't sound convinced.

So I smoked, and stared at the phone, willing the report of an arrest to come through. Just a little, Tanner's attitude troubled me, perhaps echoed a shadow of doubt of my own. Was I going too far overboard on Saxby, on the voice that matched the one I had heard so recently described? If it hadn't been his, what then? If the voice had been the killer's, then Saxby was innocent. But still it was possible I'd been talking to the sort of pest with whom investigating officers become familiar . . . or again, to a reluctant inform- ant. Why had I been so struck by that voice?

'Doesn't seem like we're going to have any luck, sir.'

In fact, even the Church Street had been a guess. And if I had let Saxby blur my vision, it meant I was neglecting angles that were perhaps more significant.

At last the phone did ring. Tanner whipped it up and listened. Then shook his head.

'We've drawn a blank, sir. Nobody like him hanging round any phone boxes.'

'No prospects sighted?'

'No, sir. They talked to a couple of girls on the prowl. One of them mentioned an old beggarman, and they found him up. But it wasn't him. Do we want them to carry on?'

I shrugged. Tanner talked instructions into the phone. I rose, and knocked my pipe out in the ashtray, looked around for my hat. Tanner lowered the phone, looked questioningly.

'I'm going for another chat with Hicks! You can turn Salmon loose for the moment, but keep a man on checking his alibi.'

'And Saxby, sir?'

'Give me a call the moment there's a sight of him.'

There was a pub across the street from the police station, and I went in for a quick pint and sandwich. Then, feeling that much more cheerful, I made my way to the lights of the Church Street. I scanned the pavements, but with little hope. If Saxby had been there he was long gone. I saw the two girls Tanner had mentioned, and one of them gave me a languishing stare; but then her companion murmured something in her ear, and the pair of them scurried away.

I crossed the street to Reydon Contracts, and at once I was aware of a change in the atmosphere. No longer were the staff standing around in groups, the word-processors idle, the reception desk unmanned. Jonesy came skating down the stairs with a file, but he affected not to see me,

71

and went on through. Janet, who'd been fiddling with a calculator at the desk, broke off to deal me a swift smile.

'Is it for Mr Hicks? You know the way, don't you?'

'You seem busy this afternoon.'

'Yes, we've got the accountants coming in.'

And she went back to tickling the calculator.

I went on up and knocked at Hicks' door, to be greeted by a surly 'Come!' I found him seated at the steel desk poring over a ledger and a cascade of print-outs. He looked up sharply as I entered. And, I thought, apprehensively.

'Oh – you. Is there any news, then?'

I pulled up a chair and sat. I said: 'We have been following up the two leads you gave us. As yet we have no conclusive results.'

'No results – not with Salmon?'

'Salmon has given us an account that we are checking.'

'You mean he has an alibi?'

'According to him, he spent yesterday evening watching television.'

'Yes – twice likely!' Hicks snorted contemptuously. 'That's as good as to say he was up to something. If you haven't guessed, he's the biggest liar since Ananias snuffed it. Have you anything on him?'

'He fits our description. Other than that, very little.'

'But you're after him.'

'We are pursuing enquiries.'

'Yes,' Hicks said. 'Yes, I can imagine.' Then he added, almost as an afterthought: 'What did you make of poor old Saxby?'

I shook my head. 'We haven't seen him yet.'

'What?'

'Saxby is missing from his home.'

'How's that, missing?'

'He went out yesterday, and so far has failed to return.'

Hicks' brown eyes peered at me. 'I don't like to hear that,' he said. 'No, I don't like it. I suppose you're not suggesting that something could have happened to him?'

'Would that be likely?'

'Well – not likely! But with these – what do you call them – introverts, you can never be quite certain.'

'Is that how you would describe Saxby?'

'Well . . . a reserved sort of bloke. Good at his job and all that, but you never knew what made him tick.'

'He'd taken a couple of hard knocks.'

Hicks nodded. 'But all the same.'

'A man perhaps ready for a desperate deed.'

'No. I can't agree with that.'

'Even . . . a tool to be used.'

Hicks' eyes hit mine. 'Good God, what are you suggesting? You've got it wrong. He isn't a Jack Salmon. He's as decent a bloke as you'll ever find. He should never have been sacked, I miss him round here, and when he turns up we're going to have him back.'

'We are?'

'We – the firm!'

'I thought it would depend on Mrs Reydon.'

'Oh damn. Oh blast.'

'So she's been round here?'

Hicks glared at the ledger. 'Yes.'

I said: 'When did she arrive?'

Hicks fretted at the ledger. 'Soon after you left. But don't get ideas – this is all above board! She paid a call to her solicitor first. She's taking over, and she can run the shop as well as her old man. And of course, she wants the accounts audited. Mrs R. is business all the way.'

'So it sounds,' I said. 'But wasn't it rather sudden?'

'Call it what you like,' Hicks said. 'Things don't stop

73

because someone snuffs it, and the sooner we're back on the ball the better.'

I said: 'We're talking about a woman who has seen her husband stabbed to death and who, at the time, appeared suitably distraught. And now, it would be less than twelve hours later, we find her in the saddle, picking up the reins. Wouldn't you call that sudden?'

Hicks riffled the ledger. 'Listen,' he said. 'Listen. You don't know the lady as well as I do, nor you don't know everything that's been going on here. Anthea had it tough. She married the boss. He promised her a partnership that never happened. She never wanted to be out of the business, but that's how it was, he wouldn't have her around here.'

'I see,' I said.

'No, you don't,' Hicks said. 'There was his cheating with all and sundry. He didn't want her round here because why? Because there's a flat upstairs where he used to take them.'

'And she knew that?'

'She must have had an idea! She'd have been there herself before they were married. But this is the point, there wasn't much left between them, and it doesn't surprise me that she isn't bowled over. I'd say divorce was on the cards, just as soon as she got hold of something that would stick.'

'She being business all the way.'

'Well, wasn't that what she was after last night?'

I paused. 'Was she?'

Hicks stroked the ledger. 'All right! Anthea told me about it when she was here.'

'Anthea told you.'

He gave me a quick look. 'And don't get ideas about that either! We worked together here for five years, she knows it's safe to talk to me.'

'About intimate matters.'

'Yes!'

'And of course, matters of business.'

He stared.

I said: 'There's so much I don't know. For example, like what you were doing last night.'

'You . . . bastard!' But the brown eyes were alarmed.

'Well?'

'I was at home. At my home in Kingston. You've only to ask.'

I nodded. 'Then perhaps I can ask you something else. When was the last time you saw Saxby?'

'What's that got to do with it?'

I shrugged.

'I don't like this,' Hicks said. 'I don't like it at all. Here am I, doing my best to be straight with you, and all you can do is ask snide questions. Next, you'll be asking if I killed Stanley.'

'And if I did?'

'I should tell you to sod off! In fact, I'm telling you to sod off anyway. I've got a business to run, things to do.'

But I didn't sod off. I said: 'This morning, you gave me the names of two credible suspects. Since then, you've had time to think about it, and I'm wondering if you've come up with anything fresh.'

He gave me a dirty look. 'Well, I haven't.'

'I'm thinking in terms of Reydon's business. People who may have lost out because of him, may even have been put out of business.'

I could see he was interested; but he shook his head. 'I could probably give you a name or two. But it's the recession that's knocked out most of them. Stanley only gave them a helping hand.'

'Perhaps a smaller, one-man business.'

'They're not the sort we have on the books. Stanley

75

always went after the big fish, the ones who could pay the fattest commissions.'

'People like Lampard.'

'Right. We fixed him up with the borough council. Before that they'd bought their supplies in dribs and drabs, but now he takes care of the lot.'

'So some smaller suppliers may have felt the draught.'

'I dare say. But that's how it goes.'

'May even have gone broke.'

'It happens. But they're not on our books, so what the hell.'

'You don't keep track of them.'

Hicks shook his head. 'There's been nothing of that sort lately, that I remember. And if there were, I wouldn't expect them to chase after Stanley with a knife. Business is business, you make it or you don't, it's no good squealing when you go bust. What we do is fair competition, and that's all there is about that.'

'So your advice is, keep after Salmon.'

'And I know what I'm talking about.' Hicks looked me in the eye.

'And . . . Saxby?'

'When you find him, tell him he's still got a job at Reydon's.'

I nodded. 'Just one more question! About an hour ago, did anyone here ring the police station?'

'Not to my knowledge. Why do you ask?'

I didn't tell him, but the background of traffic noise in the office matched that of the anonymous phone-call. On the other hand, there wasn't a trace of huskiness in Hicks' fruity, faintly cockney, accents.

Other doors besides Hicks' opened off the first-floor lounge-landing, signed variously as Records, Stationery,

Accounts and Private. Then there was another, signed S.M.R. – Knock and Wait. I paused for a moment or two, listening. Then turned the handle and went in.

In size, the office matched Hicks', but there the resemblance ended. The desk was a period piece in mahogany, the carpet underfoot of deep pile. There were club chairs, a drinks cabinet, and the window looked over a strip of garden. On the walls were a couple of paintings of nudes, just this side of pornographic. A box of Havanas lay on the desk, and a smell of stale cigar smoke hung in the air. Also, very subtly, another smell, which for the moment I couldn't identify. But then, behind a door in the corner, a cistern flushed, and the mystery fragrance was a mystery no longer. The door opened briskly, and Anthea Reydon stepped out: to halt and stare at me with widening eyes.

'What – what are you doing here!'

She was dressed today in the same severe two-piece, ruffled blouse, drab stockings and sensible, if expensive, shoes. I said:

'Forgive me if I am intruding. I had some questions for Mr Hicks. And then, to satisfy a curiosity, I ventured to step in here.'

'Did – Hicks tell you I was here?'

'Merely that you had called in earlier.'

'But you – want to see me?'

'It might be helpful. Since the opportunity arises.'

She seemed to find the prospect less than enchanting, and stared fretfully at me, at the door. But then gave a little shrug of her neat shoulders.

'Well then! I suppose we had better sit down.'

We sat; she at the desk, myself on a chair placed for interviewees. Nervously, Anthea Reydon adjusted the position of a desk calendar, squared the writing pad in front of her.

'I suppose you're surprised at finding me here, but

honestly, I couldn't just let things drift! Stanley wouldn't have wanted it, and I couldn't face going home. This seemed to be the only thing left to do. Don't you understand?'

'I must admit surprise.'

'Oh, I know! I should be acting the tearful widow. But it's still so unreal, what happened back there. Perhaps I'm in shock, but it hasn't yet hit me.'

'So instead, you are throwing yourself into the business.'

'Yes. Because I shall be running it from now on. Perhaps you haven't been told, but I was Stanley's chief assistant, I helped him to build it for five years.'

'And now you are occupying his chair.'

She squirmed. 'It's what he would have wanted!'

'Wasn't there talk of a partnership?'

Her eyes were mean. 'Hicks. Only Hicks could have told you that.'

'A partnership that didn't take place.'

'No, it didn't. And I can guess what you must be thinking. But it isn't true. I stood by Stanley. No wife could have stood by him more than I did.' She began to sniffle.

'Yet you knew he was unfaithful.'

She nodded. 'I knew.'

'And – last night?'

'I suppose it was obvious. It had gone too far. I knew I would have to do something.'

'Something . . . ?'

'Oh sod it! A divorce.'

'With a fat settlement.'

'He could afford it.'

'Yet wouldn't it have ended all your hopes of a partnership?'

'So what?'

I shook my head. 'Now, you have the lot.'

'But –!' Her stare was incredulous. 'Surely you don't

mean – you can't! I was with Phil – and that woman saw it.
And Hicks says you're after Jack Salmon.'

'A man well known to you?'

'Yes. But what –?'

'A man who might accept a proposition?'

'A man –!'

'He has a doubtful alibi. Sooner or later, we shall probably disprove it.'

Now she was sitting bolt upright. She said: 'I can't, I
won't believe I'm hearing this! That I should plot to murder
my husband – and make use of a tool like Jack Salmon? Go
ahead then – disprove his alibi! Put the bastard in the dock.
You'll hear me cheering all the way, because I've nothing to
fear from Jack Salmon.'

'Nothing to fear.'

'No!'

'From Salmon. Or any other man.'

'What other man?'

'One whom, like Salmon, your husband sacked.'

'One whom – oh no!' Her hand went to her mouth. 'Not
Henry. You can't mean him. That would be too bizarre
altogether.'

'Henry Saxby.'

'You can't be serious. Really, this is getting quite ridiculous. I was an eyewitness, remember? And that dreadful
creature wasn't Henry Saxby.'

'How can you be certain?'

'Because.' Her gaze sank from mine for a moment. 'Because he was bigger, and because ... well, the way he
moved, I suppose.'

'He was taller than Saxby?'

'Not so much that. A bigger body, more bulky. Of
course, it may have been what he was wearing, but Henry
is a slighter man, quite an elegant figure.'

'And the man you saw moved differently?'

'Differently, yes.' She shivered. 'He was violent, that's the only word. When he suddenly appeared. When he struck. And then again, when the woman shouted, and he sprang away into the alley. It couldn't have been Henry, that's absurd. I worked beside Henry all those years.'

'It more resembled someone else,' I said.

Her eyes hardened. 'Yes. And I'm prepared to say so in the witness box. That man was very much like someone else.'

'Yet . . . how far away would you have been?'

'I don't know! Fifty yards.'

'You could have glimpsed his face?'

'It was too sudden. All I could see was that terrible shape.'

'And still you are sure it wasn't Saxby?'

'How many more times must I tell you? If it was Henry, then he has changed out of all recognition since I knew him.'

I said: 'Life can sometimes change people.'

'Yes.' Anthea Reydon stared down at the desk.

I said: 'I went to his house looking for him this morning. I found there all the signs of a disintegrating personality.'

'I know, I know!' I had her eyes again. 'You don't think I played any part in that, do you? It was stupid, it was cruel, and I loathed Stanley for what he had done. I sent flowers, I went to see him, I would have helped him with money but he wouldn't take it. And it was about then that I decided I'd had enough, that I couldn't go on being Stanley's wife.'

I said: 'And have you seen Saxby since?'

'Yes. I saw him only a fortnight ago. It was out here, in the Street, and for a moment I failed to recognize him. I took him for a tramp. He wore an old coat and hat and shoes that looked as though they'd never seen polish, and his hair was down to his collar. I couldn't believe it. He used to be so meticulous.'

'Did you speak to him?'

She nodded. 'I said: "Hullo, Henry. Where are you off to?" And he mumbled something in a vague sort of way, and just carried on, as though he didn't know me. I was shocked, I can tell you. Even the way he spoke was different.'

'Yes . . . the way he spoke.'

'It was husky. As though he had a chronic cold.'

After a pause, I said: 'And since then?'

'How do you mean?'

'We are still looking for Saxby.'

'Henry is . . . missing?'

'Since lunch time yesterday. He didn't return home last night.'

Her eyes were hardening. 'And you think that I –?'

I said: 'You appear to have been a friend of his. And just now Saxby may be in need of a friend, and more than a friend. Of sanctuary.'

'And – you're looking at me?'

I was looking at her. Anthea Reydon rose to her feet. She said:

'For one day, I have been insulted enough, Superintendent. Now, you will kindly take yourself off.'

I said: 'This morning we had a certain phone-call. It was from a man with such a voice as you describe. In the background was traffic noise of a level similar to that in the office across the hall.'

Her eyes were flaming at me. 'And?'

'Above these offices, I understand there is a flat. Regrettably, before I leave, I must ask to be shown over it.'

'And should I refuse?'

'Then I shall obtain a search warrant, and meanwhile place the premises under observation.'

'Oh!' She stared furiously, helplessly. 'And it's me who has just had to watch my husband being murdered.'

81

I stared back: nodded.

'Then – then – you'd better search the rotten flat, and see if I care!'

She fumbled shakily in a drawer for her bag, and from it took a tagged key. I rose and followed her on to the lounge-landing and to the door signed Private. She unlocked it. It gave access to a half-landing on stairs from the street. We went on up. She threw open a door, and stood back, seething, for me to enter.

'I suppose you've heard all about this!'

The flat was little more than a single room, occupied mostly by a double bed and a couple of low, padded arm-chairs. Heavy curtains hung at the windows, a big sheep-skin rug covered much of the floor. The place had a close, airless atmosphere with a stale fragrance of cosmetics.

I glanced into the shower-compartment, the toilet, the bijou kitchenette. And then, for good measure, turned back the skirts of the dominating bed.

'Have I been humiliated enough?'

'I regret the need to do this, Mrs Reydon.'

'And I'm supposed to believe that – after I've been ac-cused of hiring men to do away with my husband!'

'We still need to question Henry Saxby.'

'And if I knew where he was, I wouldn't tell you.'

I said: 'I take it you do want your husband's killer to be found, Mrs Reydon?'

'Oh! Oh!' She flung away from me, and fled down the stairs.

To leave no stone unturned, I followed the stairs down to street level. But a cupboard under them, and a small entry hall, were as vacant of Saxby as the flat above.

Coming out on the crowded pavement, I almost ran into a

lounging figure. Salmon, wearing the coat that had been returned to him, was presumably on his way back to Bloemfontein Road. He dodged aside from me derisively, then halted to give me a sneering grin.

'Been up in the love-nest, have we? Let me guess, she wouldn't play!'

I looked him up and down, from head to toe. In that coat ... with a hat pulled well down ... ? I said:

'You seem familiar with the premises.'

'Beginning to get the idea?' he sneered. 'And don't tell me she never knew about it, because she'd been up there like the rest. It stands to bloody reason. You don't have to come chasing poor sods like me.'

I said: 'You are speaking of Mrs Reydon?'

'Quit kidding,' Salmon sneered. He drew closer. 'That smart-arsed bitch could have set up this job, couldn't she? He was cheating on her, right? And he was keeping her out of the business. And she's sweet on Hicky, did you know that? So bloody Reydon had to go.' He pulled back, gloatingly. 'Doesn't it fit?'

I said: 'Tell me again. Where were you last night?'

'I – what?'

'Refresh my memory. Where were you, when you weren't watching television?'

'Why, you bastard!' He took a threatening step forward, but I placed a hand on his chest, and shoved. He staggered back, stood scowling at me. But there was fear in his eyes too. 'You sod, I told you where I was.'

'Something about you and your wife, wasn't it?'

'Just try to prove different – just try.'

'Are you saying I couldn't?'

'What I'm saying –!'

But I never heard what he was saying, because at that point he broke away and hastened off. I watched him go: six feet, fair hair, hefty build and an active manner. Only the voice was wrong – could he have disguised that, to deceive Liddle?

I went back into reception to ring Tanner, but nothing fresh had come in that required my presence. He could reach me next at Bertie's Hotel, I told him. Then I winked at Janet, and took my leave.

6

'The evening paper has just come in, sir. I was hoping to see where you'd made an arrest.'

Since taking up quarters in Lime Walk, we had become *habitués* at Bertie's Hotel. A comfortable Victorian edifice on a corner site in the Church Street, it provided food that even Gabrielle could find only an occasional complaint with. In its bar it stocked my favourite bitter; it offered reliable accommodation for visiting relatives; and the rotund manager, Bushell, had become a familiar acquaintance.

'Is the private lounge available? I'd like a word with Mrs Lampard.'

'Oh dear, sir! I expect you've heard of the little upset we had here.'

'Is she in?'

'Oh yes, she's in. She hasn't stirred from her room since. She had her lunch sent up and everything – she really believes that hubby is after her!'

'Ask her to come down.'

Bushell rang her room; a degree of persuasion appeared necessary. Finally he hung up and made a pretence of mopping his brow.

'She'll be down in five minutes, sir.' He gave me a leer. 'Is her old man really the one you're after?'

I shrugged. 'That seems to be her impression.'

'More than that, sir, from what she was giving him.'

'What was she giving him?'

'Well, she swore blind that she was out there when he did it, that she saw him run after her boyfriend and slip the knife into his back. That's when he really blew his top. It took Ron and Fred and me to hold him off her. He called her every name in the book, and would have knocked her down given half a chance.' Bushell paused. 'Would it have been possible?'

'What else did Mrs Lampard say?'

'Said he'd rigged it all up with the boyfriend's wife, that she was behind it, and he was her tool. Of course, she was in a right way, she would have said anything. You couldn't depend on it for gospel. But if even half she says is right, then she's got a reason to be scared of her husband.'

'Have you seen him here since?'

Bushell shook his head. 'Your men gave him a proper rollicking. Said if they found him anywhere near the Bert again his feet wouldn't touch, he'd go straight inside. But he's been on the blower, trying to talk to her. Only the lady won't accept the calls.'

'I'll have a word with him.'

'I wish you would, sir. It's a bit uneasy, having him around.'

'In the mean time, I wouldn't pay too much attention to what may have passed between husband and wife.'

Bushell nodded. 'Got you, sir. And I'll make sure the staff keep their mouths shut. And I know you're doing your best to clear this scary business up. But there'll be faces missing from the Bert of an evening until you get that fellow behind bars.'

'I don't think your customers need fear a repetition.'

'Maybe not, sir. But that's how it goes.'

He went to attend to a guest booking out, and I made my way to the private lounge. I lit my pipe and waited. Five minutes passed, and then ten. Finally, it was twenty minutes later when Sara Lampard and her scent entered.

'Look, I want to go home and fetch some clothes, and I can't while he's still around there, can I?'

Sara Lampard was also wearing her last night's garb, except that the swagger coat had been exchanged for a cardigan.

'I shoved some undies into a bag, but I was too scared to pack properly. And it's too damned cold to go round like this. Couldn't you lock him up for just a couple of hours?'

Cosmetics she had not been too scared to pack: her face was made up with care and attention, her hair was brushed, and a miasma of Chanel accompanied her towards me. I had seated myself on one of the benches: Sara Lampard sailed up and settled herself beside me. She crossed her legs as a matter of course, and underlined the event with a twitch of her skirt. Her green-hazel eyes met mine.

'Well – couldn't you? You don't have to tell him what it's about. And after what happened here this morning he can't be surprised if you run him in.'

I shook my head. 'I'm afraid not, Mrs Lampard.'

'But I need my clothes! I'm freezing to death.'

'We can perhaps arrange to have a policewoman accompany you to your house, to fetch what you require.'

'A woman cop – what good would she be?'

'I expect to have a talk with your husband later.'

'And a fat lot of use that's going to be. Until you lock him up for keeps, I'm in trouble.' She jerked her head, and smoothed her skirt. But then she leaned a little closer. She said: 'Look, can't we get together on this? You know Phil is in this up to his neck.'

I said: 'You have something fresh to tell me?'

'Don't be so sniffy!' Mrs Lampard said. 'I want to help you, and after this morning it isn't going to break my heart to grass on Phil. He's out to get me, you know that? I've had a taste of him before. So fair's fair. Let's say I've been protecting him up to now.'

I said: 'That wasn't the case last night.'

'So last night I was giving him a hard time! But nothing I knew he couldn't talk himself out of. And that's what the so-and-so did, wasn't it?'

'You were accusing him from pique?'

'Something like that. Before he could jump on me over Stan. I thought it would give me one over him, make him think twice before he got rough.'

I shook my head. 'That wasn't how I read it.'

'I don't care! That's how it was. I thought he'd cool down, call it evens, perhaps watch how he stepped out of line in future. Well, it hasn't worked that way. So now I'm ready to play ball.'

'You are prepared to inform on him.'

'Like I said. You and me can get together on this.'

She leaned another little bit closer, and her face loomed closer still. I put a fresh light to my pipe, nullified the Chanel with a puff of Long Cut. I said:

'Perhaps we should go over your statement again. The proper setting for that is the police station.'

'Damn the police station,' Sara Lampard said. 'First, you've got to sort me out, haven't you?'

I shrugged. 'If that's what you prefer.'

'Yes, you and me together,' Sara Lampard said. 'You're the boss man on the case, aren't you? So now you just ask me what you want to know.'

I puffed. 'Then from the beginning,' I said. 'From the evening you spent in the company of the victim.'

Sara Lampard winced. 'Do I get a drink?'

I reached for the button, and pressed.

She ordered a gin and lime, and I ordered a simple coffee. Bushell himself served, and took the opportunity to give me a knowing wink over Sara Lampard's head. Then, on leaving, he closed the door with an almost tangible discreetness. Sara Lampard sipped silently for a spell. She seemed to find it difficult to begin.

'Look, about Stanley! I don't want you to think he was ever the great love of my life. It was how I told you, I liked his style, but that's how it was. We weren't going anywhere.'

I said: 'Last night I received a different impression.'

'So what did you bloody well expect! He'd just had a knife stuck in him, hadn't he, and I was still woozy from carrying on with him. No, he was just my little ray of sunshine, a bit of goods that I could depend on. And the same with him. Little Mrs bored him, he needed some glam to cheer him up.'

'A pact of mutual convenience.'

'Well, a girl gets bored too, doesn't she? Especially married to a louse like Philip, who only has time for his rotten business. So that's it, that's how it was. We weren't going to hurt anyone. And that's how it would have gone on if Little Mrs hadn't let on to Phil.'

'You suspect her of telling him.'

'Must have done. Phil never got a smell of it from us. Before last night we always met in the flat, the one Stan had over his office. But last night, of course, those two devils let us think we'd got it made, so he came to my place, and all the while they were sitting outside, waiting for him.'

'What time did he arrive?'

'Six, or after. Like I said, I had a meal ready.'

'Did he mention encountering anyone on the way to yours?'

Sara Lampard stared. 'How do you mean?'

89

'Perhaps someone with whom he may have been acquainted.'

She kept staring, but shook her head. 'No. And if he'd spotted those two, he wouldn't have come to the house at all. He'd have kept going, perhaps come here, and given me a ring to let me know what was cooking. And me, I'd have shoved that grub in the dustbin and settled down with a good book.'

'Specifically, did he mention any ex-employees?'

'Why the hell should he want to talk about them?'

'Did he?'

'No he didn't. And we didn't talk about football or cricket either.'

'You enjoyed an undisturbed evening.'

'You could put it like that.'

'For example, no callers. Nobody on the phone.'

'If there were, I shouldn't think we would have heard them.'

'Then perhaps we can get on to what happened later.'

She drank up, set her glass on the table. She wasn't staring at me now. After a moment, she brushed her skirt thoughtfully; revealing another inch of leg. She said:

'I had to shove him out, didn't I? He was one of them who can never have enough. But come eleven he had to go, because Phil is never home much later than that.'

'You saw him out.'

'Yes.'

I said: 'Naturally, you would glance up the Walk. To see who was about.'

'Yes, we did. And there was no one. Just the parked cars and nothing else.'

'You kissed him good-night.'

She nodded.

'And then you went in. To put on the coffee.'

90

She stroked her skirt again, and then, very delicately, shook her head.

'You – didn't go in?'

'No. Wouldn't be much good to you if I had done, would I?'

I said: 'Did you or didn't you?'

'No. I just told you that to protect Phil.'

It was my turn to stare, and I stared. Sara Lampard kept her eyes on the table. Though earlier she had complained about the cold, there was a flush in her painted cheeks now. I said:

'Go on.'

'Yes, well. I wanted to see him safely on his way, didn't I? So I hung on a bit. I hadn't put the hall light on. I thought I'd just see him clear of the house.'

'Even though your husband was momentarily expected?'

'I'd have heard his car coming in from the Church Street.'

'The coffee could wait?'

'Sod it, yes! I'd left it all ready to switch on.'

'So?'

She traced a line on her skirt. 'So I saw him off. Maybe half-way towards his house. Then I heard a car door across the street. So I slipped back into the hall.'

'And, of course, closed the door.'

'Don't be daft. I wanted to see who it was. I kept the door just ajar, so I could close it quickly if I had to. At first I couldn't make them out, they were behind the cars on the other side, but then they came under a street light and I could see it was Phil and Little Mrs Butter.'

'On the side opposite to Reydon.'

'Yes, and they were hurrying along to catch him up. I didn't know whether to shout, or what to do. Of course, I couldn't guess what was going to happen.'

I said: 'So what did happen?'

91

Sara Lampard traced lines. She said: 'I think she tried to stop him, she hung on to his arm. But he pulled away.'

'Him being your husband?'

'Yes! And he had something in his hand. He pulled away and sneaked after Stanley, keeping crouched and behind the cars.'

'Wouldn't Reydon have heard something?'

'Well, he didn't. He just kept walking towards his house. And Phil, he sneaked across the road . . . you don't need me to tell you what happened next.'

I said: 'I think you had better.'

Sara Lampard tossed her head. She said: 'It was all confused, wasn't it, and me right down there at the other end. But I saw him hit Stanley, I can tell you that. And Stanley yelled out and fell down. I thought Phil had hit him with a stone or something, I didn't know till later that he'd been stabbed. So what was I to do? Phil had stopped hitting him, and Little Mrs Butter was on the job. I decided I was better off inside, you know, until the heat was off a bit.'

I said: 'In your mind, there is no doubt that your husband struck the blow?'

'No. I saw him do it, didn't I?'

'At a distance of, say, one hundred and fifty yards. And in a poorly lit street?'

'There was only him and Stan up there, and I'd been watching him all the way.'

I said: 'We do have another witness.'

'Another witness – you mean Little Mrs?'

I shook my head. 'An independent witness. One who saw the blow being struck.'

'Oh . . . I see. And what do they say?'

I said: 'They say this. That the man who struck Reydon came from behind the tree standing there. And that after he struck the blow, he ran off into the mews.'

Sara Lampard stared at her glass. Then shrugged. She

said: 'Well, it might have looked like that to someone! As I said, it was all confused, someone else may have seen it different. Will that be a problem?'

'I think it may be.'

'But I'm his bloody wife! They must believe me.'

'That may just be the problem.'

'But we can get round it!'

I stared into the green-hazel eyes. 'No.'

'What do you mean – no?'

I said: 'As a liar, Mrs Lampard, you are probably in a class of your own. But I think we must stick with the statement you signed. And I would advise you to do so too.'

She didn't strike me: she was a woman of character; but her eyes were telling me to drop dead. For a brief spell we stared at each other in the smoky silence of the lounge. Was Bushell hovering behind the door? Subduedly, one heard the business of the hotel proceeding, a distant voice in conversation, a muffled bell, the thud of swing doors. Then, suddenly, the staring eyes were beseeching. And a crimson-taloned hand pressed my knee.

'Look – you don't have to be like that! I'm trying to help you, can't you understand? We can get together on this. You only have to treat me as half-way human.'

I removed the hand. 'I'm sorry.'

'I was there. You can't deny that! And only I know how much I saw. Why can't we just take it from there?'

I shook my head.

'But yes. This other witness – look, we can get round that. I keep telling you, it was all confused. They may have seen one thing, and me another. What's wrong with that?'

'Just about everything.'

'But you can't have to be so bloody particular! I'm a

witness, and you've got to accept me. How else are you ever going to sew this up?'

I merely shook my head again. She grabbed my arm. She said:

'You've got to! You must give me a chance.'

'A chance . . . ?'

'It may not stick, but you can give it a go.'

'You mean, arrest your husband on false testimony?'

'But you don't know it's false!'

I said: 'I, too, was there.'

'Oh, sod it!' Her eyes flashed afresh, but almost immediately softened again. She said: 'Look, we can talk this over somewhere else, we don't have to stick in this stupid room.'

I said: 'We've already talked it over.'

'I could haul my pants down and holla rape!'

'No, Mrs Lampard.'

'Then what am I going to do? Because that rotten bastard is going to get me in the end.' Now her face suddenly crumpled, and for once I didn't think she was acting. She dropped my arm, hugging herself, and tears began to mingle with mascara. She said: 'He did it. I'm blind bloody certain. He said he would do for the next one he caught with me. I didn't believe him, but he meant it. And now it's my turn. He'll do me next.'

'Perhaps you behaved a little foolishly, Mrs Lampard.'

'Yes – I let him know I knew it was him!'

'He would, of course, be incensed.'

'He was ready to bloody strangle me. He's probably hanging about outside there now.'

I said: 'Had there, then, been many others?'

She snuffled. 'Perhaps one or two.'

'Any recently?'

'You know how it is. I'm on my own all day, and sometimes half the night.'

'During your liaison with Reydon?'

Her shoulders humped.

I said: 'Does this suggest anything to you: a man in his forties, six foot, powerful build, fair hair and grey-blue eyes?'

She stared muzzily through tears. 'You louse. I know the one you mean.'

'An ex-employee of Reydon's?'

'Jackie Salmon. What the hell has he got to do with it?'

'But he was your lover?'

Her eyes sparked again. 'Just never you mind! I've had enough of this. The point is what you're going to do about Philip, not who I've been jumping in and out of bed with.'

I shrugged. 'We shall certainly speak to him.'

'You won't bloody arrest him?'

'I can't promise that.'

'Then what happens to me?'

I said: 'Perhaps an apology. And a promise of more discretion during encounters in public?'

'Oh, you sod!' She jumped to her feet, and this time seemed really likely to strike me. She didn't. She flounced out of the lounge, almost into the arms of a grinning Bushell.

'I thought you might have been in need of the marines, sir!'

I grimaced, and asked him to call me a taxi. I rang Lampard's office. A cockney voice told me yes, Mr Lampard was about the yard somewhere. A second ring, to the police station, brought news of some interesting progress: Donna, Mrs Salmon, had been seen in the Church Street at around eight p.m. the previous evening.

'So she couldn't have been at home all the time, sir. At least, she may have popped out for a pint.'

'Check the pubs.'

'We're doing that, sir. It's a job that nobody minds.'

Salmon . . . Saxby . . . or was it still just possible? The taxi dropped me at Hagg Lane, in the Bush. It was a depressing thoroughfare, not far from the football ground, and invested largely with yards and sheds. Lampard's was the most extensive of these. It stretched along all one side of the lane: dumps of timber, bricks, breeze-blocks, backed by warehouses of corrugated asbestos. At the gate was an unimpressive office building, and parked beside it a maroon Mercedes. I went in. Behind a counter, a man in dungarees was pencilling a list.

'Mr Lampard?'

'Upstairs, squire. But he isn't seeing any reps today.'

Notwithstanding, I went on up, and knocked at the principal door I found there. An irascible voice bade me enter. Lampard was standing at a window, staring out at the yard.

'If you've come to arrest me, I wouldn't blame you. I know you've been talking to my wife.'

Lampard was looking haggard, his eyes baggy, a droop in the corners of his thin mouth. He'd shown no surprise when he turned from the window, just given me a long, silent stare. Then he'd sat himself down at a desk loaded with dog-eared forms and dockets.

'You went to Bertie's Hotel, didn't you? Anthea gave me a ring from Reydon's. And if you believe half of what Sara's been telling you, then you'll have come with a warrant in your pocket. Am I wrong?'

'May I sit down?'

'Just get it over, that's all I ask! Even the staff here think I've done it. They know the story, every last one.'

I removed box-files from a chair, hitched it across to the

96

desk and sat. Lampard watched me with wretched eyes. I wondered how much sleep he'd had last night. I said:

'That was an unwise thing you did this morning.'

'Oh yes! You'll have heard all about that too. And that's the last straw, isn't it? You think I went there to terrorize a witness.'

'Why did you go?'

'You'll never believe me, but I went to try to make it up with Sara. Perhaps the poor bitch didn't deserve it, but she must have had a hell of a shock last night. You were there, you saw her. She was going spare. She isn't as tough as she likes to make out. And when that happens she can go to pieces. So I went round to try to calm her down.'

'Just that?'

Lampard stared bitterly. 'Of course, you're never going to understand! You haven't lived with Sara like I have, and it suits you to take her at face value. Down there, under-neath, she's a scared woman – and I don't mean just scared of me! It's happened before. She's had breakdowns. It began when we discovered she couldn't have children. And that's what this thing with other blokes is about, she's trying all the time to prove that she's a woman. It doesn't work, I try to protect her, that's what it was about last night. Only now she's convinced I went the whole way and made bloody certain she was finished with Reydon.' His stare was anguished. 'Can't you understand that?'

I said: 'She certainly spoke with conviction.'

'Oh yes – I'd barely got through the door this morning when she was screaming that I was a killer! So I lost my temper, I'm sorry, it was the worst thing I could have done. And now she's doubly convinced, and probably has managed to convince you. Isn't that why you're here?'

I shrugged.

'You're going to believe her – and not me and Anthea?'

'We have to pursue each line of an enquiry.'

97

'Yes,' Lampard said. 'Yes. I can bloody imagine.'

A hooter sounded down in the yard, and Lampard swung round to glare through the window. A large truck was backing up to a warehouse; Lampard watched till it was safely parked. He turned back to me. I said:

'Last night, you saw Reydon take leave of your wife.'

'Am I supposed to go through all that again?'

'If you will.'

Lampard looked mean. 'I thought they were never going to break it up.'

'You could see them clearly?'

'Too damned clearly! So could anyone else, if they'd been there. She came to the door with him, and he grabbed her. Ask Anthea. It made both of us sick.'

'Yet the street lighting there is poor.'

'So what? There was the light from the house.'

'You mean the hall light?'

'Well, yes. They had the hall light behind them, didn't they?'

'They could be seen in silhouette.'

'Yes, I'm telling you.'

'Visible to anyone in the Walk.'

'The whole damned neighbourhood could have seen them. They didn't seem to give a monkey's eff.'

'And, when they broke up?'

'How do you mean?'

'Was the light behind him when he walked away?'

'No, of course not. She'd nipped in pronto, to make like she'd spent the evening watching telly. When I got back there everything was tidy, not a dirty cup or glass in the place. The telly was still switched on, and the coffee percolator still warm. I was to walk in to find an ever-loving wife, with coffee on the go for a fagged-out hubby.'

I nodded. 'Let's take it from there.'

Lampard eyed me doubtfully. 'Well, we got out and followed him.'

'You gave him a start.'

'Of course we did! It wasn't the idea to have a row in the street. We were going to follow him back home, and have it out with him there. Then I was going to have it out with Sara. That was how it had been planned.'

'You saw no one else at all in the Walk.'

'No. There'd been no one about for half an hour.'

'Go on.'

'What more can I tell you? It's all down there in the statement I gave you.'

'Still, carry on.'

Lampard hunched his broad shoulders. 'So we followed him. On the other side. We'd been quiet about closing the car doors, so I don't think he knew we were there. Anyway, he didn't look back, and the parked cars would probably have hidden us. He got to his house, was just turning towards the steps. Then this fellow sprang out from nowhere.'

'From the shadow of the tree.'

'That's where he must have been. But it all happened so quickly. We heard the thud as he hit Reydon, and Reydon scream. Then the fellow was away.'

'Mrs Cartwright shouted.'

'I'm not sure if I heard her. For a moment I was simply staggered. Then I was running like crazy towards Reydon. I still think he could have been alive when I reached him.'

'And pulled the knife out.'

'All right! What the devil would you have done, in my place? But then I could sense he'd had it, it was like pulling something out of dead meat. He was gone.'

'And the man you saw?'

'We only had that one glimpse of him. And by then he was long gone, and I was having to support Anthea.'

'Nothing struck you about him as familiar?'

'Good God, no. Nothing.'

'Six feet, hefty build, perhaps fair hair?'

Lampard stared, but shook his head.

I said: 'Going back to six months ago! You entertained Reydon and his staff at a celebration party. I believe that was where Reydon met your wife. Were there any other men there in whom she showed an interest?'

Lampard scowled. 'Wasn't Reydon enough?'

'I'm thinking of two men who Reydon subsequently sacked.'

'Oh . . . yes. I did hear he'd sacked a bloke called Salmon. It hadn't to do with Sara, had it?'

'Nothing. But would you remember him?'

'I shouldn't think so,' Lampard said. 'I shook hands with them all round, but Hicks is the only one who sticks in my memory.'

'Perhaps a Henry Saxby?'

'Sorry. No.'

I said: 'Then that's just about all, Mr Lampard.'

'You mean . . . you aren't going to arrest me?'

I shook my head. 'But there is one incidental matter. Your wife.' His eyes went still. I said: 'She is a very frightened woman, Mr Lampard. Just now, you perhaps shouldn't try to see her, or even to talk to her on the phone. Also, she left home in rather a hurry, and she's too scared to return for some things she needs. I would like to ring and assure her that, for say the next three hours, you promise to remain in your office here. May I do that?'

'The poor bloody bitch . . .'

'Is that your assent?'

He pushed the phone towards me. Outside, the hooter sounded again, but this time Lampard remained staring at nothing in particular.

7

For no especial reason I had the taxi set me down again in the Church Street, where now, in the frosty gloom of late afternoon, the Christmas lights sparkled even brighter.

Was I expecting something to happen? I strolled slowly by the foyer of Bertie's, eyeing the throng of pedestrians, casting a glance at reception. The same at Reydon's. There I caught the enquiring eye of Jonesy, who had paused to chat with Janet, still with a batch of files clutched under his arm.

Nearby a bus was setting down passengers, and a car had paused illegally to pick one up. And a broad-shouldered figure in a misted phone box turned to reveal the features of our local fishmonger. I shrugged to myself: nothing happening! Just the Street going about its pre-Christmas business. Yet that feeling persisted, that something was afoot there, perhaps a sign that I was failing to pick up . . .

And then I spotted him, just as I was about to turn off to head for the police station: a shabby, shambling figure on the opposite side of the street. He'd been watching me, doubtless the reason for the feeling I had experienced; and now, finding my eyes upon him, he turned abruptly and vanished into an opening. The traffic swirled by. I was stuck on my side. It may have been a minute before I could cross. By then, the yard on which the opening gave was deserted, and likewise the lane to which it had access.

Swearing under my breath, I hastened back to the Street and to the nearest vacant phone box. I rang Tanner. I said:

'I think I may have spotted Saxby, but he was away before I could grab him. He's in the area of Opie Yard and Skinner's Lane, and I want patrols out there double-quick.'

For some reason, Tanner hesitated. He said: 'You mean right here in Kensington, sir?'

'Yes, right here!'

'Well, I don't know, sir. But I've just sent them out to the Chelsea Embankment.'

'What!'

'We've had another of those calls, you know, the bloke with the hoarse voice. He said if we wanted Saxby, that was where we could pick him up. I tried to get in touch with you at Lampard's, but by then you were on your way.' Tanner paused. 'Are you certain it was Saxby you spotted just now, sir?'

I scowled at myself in the mirror. 'That call could have been a hoax!'

'Well, yes, sir . . .'

'And Saxby could have made it – from this same box I'm standing in now.'

'Yes, he could . . .'

'So let's have some action. The man I saw answers Saxby's description – five-ten or eleven, fifties, dark-coloured shabby coat and a battered hat.'

'And . . . the Chelsea bit, sir.'

'Keep it going. Just in case there's something in it.'

I hung up and left the box, went back to mount guard on that too-convenient opening. But my hopes were receding. Saxby, if it were he, had had plenty of time to make good his retreat. He knew the area and his recent wanderings would have helped perfect that knowledge, while it required only the next bus or tube to remove him from the scene completely. And then . . . the phone calls.

102

An innocent man?

The pendulum was swinging back in his direction.

When the patrols came I left it with Pyatt and made my way back to the police station. Tanner was on the phone when I entered his office, and he hung up with a smirk of satisfaction.

'Don't know about Saxby, sir,' he said. 'But Salmon's coming to hand like a pint pot. That was Thurloe on the blower. He says Donna Salmon was playing the joanna in The Black Boys last night. That was between eight and nine. Do you reckon Liddle could have got it wrong?'

I shrugged, and related what I had unearthed about a possible liaison between Salmon and Sara Lampard. Tanner's eyes glistened.

'That would put jam on it, if Reydon was cutting him out with Mrs L.! Is that how you see it, sir?'

'It fits together. And he could have witnessed their torrid embrace at parting. That could have been the final straw.'

'I love it,' Tanner said. 'It's beautiful.'

'But then we come up against Wilfred Liddle.'

Tanner looked down his nose. 'It was the voice he was going on,' he said. 'Liddle did pick Salmon out in the line-up, and Salmon could have faked his voice when he was buying that knife.'

'As well as dressing like a tramp?'

'I don't see why not. I'd say the two went together. Salmon was out to do a proper job, and like it was good enough to fool Liddle.'

'A proper job.' I shook my head. 'Would you credit Salmon with that much intelligence?'

'It wouldn't need so much, sir.'

'It probably wouldn't have occurred to him that we could trace the knife back to Liddle in the first place.'

103

'Well . . . if you put it like that!'

'Also the voice. I doubt if Salmon would be capable of faking it. Imitating hoarseness isn't easy. And it certainly wasn't Salmon I spoke to on the phone.'

Tanner frowned. 'I have to admit that, sir. It wasn't him I was talking to just now. That bloke really has a graveyard sound, like he'd been sleeping rough for weeks.'

'What exactly did he say?'

'First he asked for you, sir. He seemed put out because you weren't here. Then he said: "Tell him that if he wants Saxby, he'll find him on the Embankment down Chelsea way." So I said: "Who shall I say called?" – but he just breathed a bit heavy, and hung up.'

'Background traffic noises?'

'Now you mention it. Do you reckon it could be someone having a game?'

I shook my head. 'And I doubt if it's Saxby, wanting to give himself up.'

'So if it isn't Salmon, who's the bloke?'

I said: 'We need a sample of that voice! It may be he won't risk another call, but if he does, I want it on tape. See to it, will you?'

'Right away,' Tanner said. 'We could try it on Liddle for a start.'

He went out. I lit my pipe. Was it just possible that we had a third prospect? Lampard I felt sure we might eliminate. Salmon fitted so well, but there were gaps. And Saxby . . . ? The pendulum was swinging, but who was it trying to give the pendulum a nudge? Tanner came back smirking. He said:

'Right you are, sir! I'm afraid the bloke you spotted was a have. The boys have just come in from Chelsea, and they've got Saxby nestling in the back of their car.'

Quite elegant was how Anthea Reydon had described the build of Henry Edward Saxby, but if so it was not apparent in the figure now hustled into Tanner's office. Saxby looked a mess. He was bundled up in a coat that might have seen service in the Crimea, swathed in a muffler to his ears, with an old stained trilby dragged down to meet it. He was wearing shoes that looked sodden and the cuffs of his trousers were plated with mud. He hadn't shaved lately, or washed, and a sort of dampness clung to his whole person. I pointed to a chair, said:

'When was the last time you ate, Saxby?'

'I . . . yesterday . . . it may have been . . .'

It was a whispering croak: but not the voice on the telephone.

I ordered sandwiches and tea to be fetched. Saxby sat down gingerly, as though something might break. Divested of the hat, he looked slightly more human, though his uncombed grey hair sadly needed a trim. He had narrow but well-formed features and pale brown eyes that were staring at nothing. Though it was warm in the office he made no attempt to unbutton his coat.

'Do you smoke, Saxby?'

'I . . . no . . .'

Tanner was watching him with an avuncular fondness, an affection almost. Edith, who had brought him in, stood staring at Saxby with twitching nostrils.

The tray came. I let Saxby eat and drink without interruption. He crammed sandwiches into his mouth with a sort of mechanical avidity. The plate was soon cleared: he drank, burped, then hooked the muffler away from his chin. Finally, if he didn't exactly look at me, he let his empty eyes turn in my direction.

I said: 'You know why your presence is required here, Saxby?'

For reply he dug into a pocket of his coat. Out came a

dishevelled copy of the lunch-time paper: it carried the banner headline: BUSINESSMAN STABBED.

'Have you anything to say?'

'No . . . I . . .'

'Why have you not come forward before?'

His eyes were levelled at my chest, but nothing escaped from his trembling lips.

I said: 'You have been absent from your home since lunch time yesterday. You must have known we would want to speak to you. Yet you appear to have been avoiding encountering us. What do you expect us to make of that, Saxby?'

'I . . . I didn't . . .'

'Well?'

'I didn't . . .' His voice was a whisper.

'You wish to say you didn't attack Stanley Reydon?'

'No . . . no. I didn't . . .'

I stared at those unseeing eyes for a moment. 'Very well. Your answer is noted, Saxby. But what we want to know now is what you were doing between lunch time yesterday and say, midnight last night. Where were you, during that time?'

The trembling lips struggled.

'Well?'

'If I could . . .'

'Yes?'

'Something . . . just a little . . . to drink?'

'To drink . . . ?' I looked at Tanner.

'Oh, I think we can manage that, sir!' Tanner said. 'A little drop we keep by for emergencies. Edith, look in my private locker.'

So a glass of brandy was produced, and Saxby drank it in trembling sips. It brought a slight flush to his bristly cheeks, and a growing focus to his vacant eyes. Finally he put the glass down. He said:

'I might . . . it might. I don't know . . .'

'You – don't know.'

'No. Ada . . .' He made an effort to keep his lips from trembling. 'When . . . since then . . . I don't remember everything that happens. I hate the house. I can't bear it. I only go back there to sleep. Or not then. I've been out before . . . all night. Perhaps longer . . .'

'You stay out all night?'

'All night . . . yes. When I can't face going home. Sometimes, it seems . . .' He grabbed the glass and swallowed the last drains.

I said: 'Where do you go?'

'I go anywhere. The streets . . . And Walham Green, I go there. We used to live there, in Oakley Street. So I go to see our old house, how it used to be then . . . only now they've put cladding on it, and one of those fancy doors.'

I said: 'You would know where Reydon lived?'

'Yes. He'd moved there before . . .'

'And you've been round that way?'

'Yes . . . once. But last night I don't think . . .'

'Then where did you go last night?'

Saxby's eyes almost met mine. But not for long. He said: 'The streets . . . somewhere. I just went.'

'You just went?'

His head sank. 'I couldn't stand it. I had to go. Suddenly, that house . . . Anywhere seems closer to her than there. So it hits me and I have to go. Anywhere . . . it doesn't matter.'

I said: 'So then you could have been anywhere.'

'Yes. Anywhere at all.'

'For example, around six p.m. yesterday you could have been seen in Hammersmith Broadway.'

'I . . . where?'

I merely stared. Hadn't something flickered in those downcast eyes? After a moment, Saxby said:

'No, I'm certain. I didn't go in that direction at all.'

'Anywhere, but not Hammersmith?'

'No. I'm sure I would have remembered.'

'So a witness who said he saw you there would be lying?'

'He – he would have to be mistaken.'

'Say a small shopkeeper. On the point of closing. Who sold you a certain item, last thing?'

'But I didn't buy anything!'

'He gave us your description.'

'But I tell you again – I wasn't there!'

'And – if he picks you out in a line-up?'

Saxby's voice was getting hoarser by the minute. And at last I did have his eyes – baffled, fearful, just a shade indignant.

'He can't, because I wasn't there. I haven't been Hammersmith way for a week. I – I was down Cromwell Road way, I think. But at this end, not down there.'

'Cromwell Road way.'

'Yes. I think.'

'In fact, quite a step from Lime Walk.'

'I was never in Lime Walk!'

I held his eyes. 'And if another witness says you were?'

'Then – then they're lying too!' But he couldn't keep his eyes facing mine.

To Tanner I said: 'Let's have some more tea up.' Edith fetched in steaming mugs. Saxby took his in a shaky hand, swallowed mouthfuls in gulps. The hot tea made his eyes water and he was having to blink away tears. In the end, he fetched out a filthy handkerchief and surreptitiously dabbed at his eyes. I said:

108

'You've been having a bad time, Saxby. This morning I visited your house. I talked to your neighbour there. She gave me an idea of the way you've been living. It's been going on for how long, now?'

Saxby stared, but didn't answer. I said:

'For six weeks, anyway, you've been in this state. What happened must have hit you very, very hard.'

Saxby whimpered and gulped tea. I said:

'I saw that photograph of your wife. There was a great tenderness in her smile. How long ago since it was taken?'

'Oh no . . . please!'

'A recent picture?'

'Please, no . . .'

'Was it this year?'

'No . . . no.'

'Then when was it taken?'

Now the tears he was dabbing were too real. He said:

'This year . . . just before . . .'

'Before she was stricken?'

He nodded. 'We went to Bournemouth for the weekend. One of those breaks you see advertised. She had it taken . . . I don't know! And it was when we came back . . .'

'You think she may have guessed?'

'I can't talk about it!'

'But it was soon after that?'

He sobbed: 'A fortnight. The doctor rushed her into St Stephen's. But she didn't last more than a week, and half the time she couldn't . . .'

'You saw her each day?'

'Yes. The last two nights I spent up there. Then . . . I can't go on! I was kept away when she went.'

'You were kept away.'

'Yes. He told me my job was on the line. But in the end I went anyway . . . only it was too late. Ada had gone.'

'And you did lose your job.'

109

'I didn't care. What did it matter any more? Nothing mattered. Nothing. She was gone. Ada was gone.'

'And . . . all that happened three months ago.'

'I don't know. I haven't counted.'

'For three months you've lived this impotent existence, roaming the streets like any tramp.'

'I tell you it doesn't matter!'

'A broken man. An impotent man. While he who kept you from your dying wife and brutally sacked you – flourished.'

'I didn't – I can't –!' He sobbed unashamedly. 'All right, all right – I hated Reydon! I could have done it, could have killed him. If I'd met him with a gun in my hand, I would have shot him.'

'Only you didn't have a gun.'

'I'd have shot him! It was him or me, you understand? I wanted to kill myself too, in the river, or under a bus. But then, why should it be me? I was the victim, the one he'd wronged. Perhaps I did kill him and don't remember, I don't know. It must be possible.'

'Did you kill Reydon, Saxby?'

'It's possible, isn't it? And I wouldn't remember?'

'But did you?'

'I can't remember!'

'Saxby, did you?'

He sobbed. 'No.'

I said: 'Then last night, where would you have been?'

He dabbed his eyes wretchedly. 'Around.'

'You told me the Cromwell Road.'

'I – I was there later. I was on my way to the river.'

'Later than what?'

'Just later! I didn't notice where I was. Maybe Kensington High at one time. But what I was thinking of was the river.'

'The High – but not the Church Street?'

'No.'

110

'You were never closer to Lime Walk than the High?'

'I never was, nor I wasn't in Hammersmith, whatever you're getting people to say.'

'Then you'll be willing to stand in a line-up?'

He sniffed into the handkerchief. 'It won't prove anything.'

'But you are willing?'

He sniffed a few more times before replying: 'If I must.'

I sipped my own tea, which had grown cold. I said: 'Tell me, Saxby. Do you have any enemies?'

'Any . . . ?'

I said: 'I think I should tell you this. We have had two phone-calls earlier today. One of them accused you of the crime in Lime Walk, and the other told us we could pick you up in Chelsea. Would you know who the caller might be?'

I had Saxby's full attention now! The pale eyes stared at me, the crusted lips gaped. He said:

'But who –?'

'It was the voice of a man. A voice just as husky as your own.'

'But it wasn't me!'

'Clearly, he knew you. He also knew why you would interest us.'

'But there isn't anyone –'

'In addition, he seems to have tracked you down to Chelsea.'

Saxby's stare was frightened. 'But there was no one about there! I'd been down on the shore since this morning. All I saw was a down-and-out who stuck his head over the wall for a moment.'

'A down-and-out?'

'That's what he looked like.'

'Can you describe the man?'

'No! I only saw his head and shoulders for an instant, and why should I want to stare at him?'

111

'So you didn't recognize him?'

'No. But what can he possibly have against me?'

'Perhaps – an ex-colleague?'

'No.' He hung on for a moment. 'No. He just looked like a down-and-out.'

'In fact . . . a bit like you.'

'Well . . . I suppose so! He'd got his collar about his ears, and an old hat pulled right down. But I can't tell you any more than that.'

I hesitated, then let it go. I said: 'Then that's all for the moment, Saxby. We shall require a written statement from you, and after that you will be asked to take your place in a line-up.'

'Yes . . . but who was that man?'

It was indeed the question. I was almost beginning to feel that he might be familiar.

The line-up was conducted under modest floodlighting, which was probably ideal from Liddle's point of view; duplicating the conditions of the previous evening, when he'd struck that hasty bargain with an apparent beggar. Since few of the volunteers were wearing coats the line-up shivered in suits and sweaters, but sufficient head-gear had been assembled, though none of it matched Saxby's sweat-stained trilby. Beneath his coat, surprisingly, he was wearing a quite-presentable suit, even if the trousers were mud-stained below, and the effect qualified by a greasy muffler. He chose a position in the middle of the line, stood head bowed, shivering patiently. Liddle was called.

'Same routine as before.'

This time Liddle seemed to treat it as a challenge. He lingered frowningly before each prospect, peered into each face, stood back to weigh them up. And he liked Saxby. He liked his shoes, the muddied trousers, the trilby. Almost, he raised his hand to touch him. But then he let it drop again.

'That geezer . . .'

'You wish to hear his voice?'

The process was gone through again with Saxby. Obediently, in his husky whisper, he enquired the price of the doggie in the window.

'Could he do it again?'

Saxby did so. All the time Liddle was peering into his face. Then he stepped back to eye him up and down; but finally, reluctantly, began to shake his head. He drew me aside.

'It's no go, squire! He's near enough, but it wasn't him. My man had a deeper voice, and his chops were different, not so thin.'

'You can describe the face?'

'Naow! But looking at him, I know it's wrong. This other bloke's was wider, and there was something about his nose.'

'What about it?'

'Don't know, do I? But it wasn't like this bloke's here.'

'Hooked? Snubbed?'

'It's no good, squire. All I know is it wasn't him.'

And that was the best to be got out of Liddle. I thanked and dismissed him. Saxby was fetched back into the office. He dragged his coat back on his shivering body and stood staring at me as he fumbled with the buttons. He quavered:

'Who was he . . . that man?'

'It doesn't matter.'

'But he was supposed to recognize me, wasn't he?'

I said: 'Sit down, Saxby, and listen to what I have to say.' After a pause, he sank on a chair. I said: 'Between you and me, I think you could be more helpful, Saxby. I am not convinced that you can really be so vague about your movements last night. But, for the moment, we'll leave it at that.

113

Shortly, you will be free to go. What you will not be free to do is to absent yourself from this neighbourhood. You will go home, and you will stay there, and hold yourself available to this inquiry. If you do not, you will be arrested. Do you understand what I'm telling you?'

'Yes, but that other man . . . the one on the phone!'

'I don't think you need to worry about him.'

'But if he's trying to make you believe . . .'

I shook my head. 'You'll do best to forget him.' I paused. 'Unless you can tell me who he is?'

'No, of course not. But . . .'

'Then you can leave that man to us. And meanwhile, I have a message for you. From Mr Hicks of Reydon Contracts.'

'From . . . Hicky?'

I nodded. 'He wishes you to call in at the office. And if you will accept a word of advice, you will smarten up a little before you go there.'

I left him staring, and beckoned Tanner to accompany me out of the office. I said: 'Have we a man available? I want Saxby tailed from the moment he walks out of here.'

'Yes sir – that's what I was thinking!'

'Six feet, fair hair, hefty build, broad features and a prominent nose.'

'And knows all about Saxby, sir. It's only that voice that gets in the way.'

I said: 'So let's not be too hasty. Just have a good man following Saxby.'

'But you must admit, it does add up, sir . . . we could have a man in the cell tonight!'

DC Cresswell was the tail deputed, and after he was briefed I dismissed Saxby. The ex-clerk left without another word, though perhaps looking a little less shattered than when he arrived. Tanner saw him go with thoughtful eyes. He said:

114

'I don't know what to think about him, sir! At times I was taking him for real, at other times he struck me as being a bit clever.'

'Perhaps a bit of both.'

'Yes, sir. We might even wind up with him after all. But he was hiding something, that's my opinion. We're not at the bottom of Saxby yet.'

I shrugged, and reached for the phone to ring Gabrielle, but as I reached for it, it rang. I hooked it up, and at once I was hearing the familiar background of passing traffic. I said briskly:

'Gently here.'

A sound of hoarse breathing. Then: 'So you let him go, did you? You aren't going to buy bloody Saxby.'

I said: 'Why not come in and discuss it?'

More of the ragged breathing. Then: 'I can see I'll have to grass on an old mate, shan't I?' – and the phone was immediately hung up.

Tanner was already on his feet. He jerked: 'Was that chummie?'

'Yes – and he can't be far away. He's just seen Saxby leaving the station.'

'Why, the cheeky so-and-so –!'

Tanner rushed out, and I could hear him shouting orders. I went to the window. Just down the street, on the opposite side, I could see a phone box. A uniform man was dashing across to it; but the box, alas, was empty. Other uniform men arrived and ran up and down the pavement, stopped passers-by, poked into unlit doorways. Then they began to spread out and cast about, or stood staring suspiciously at surprised pedestrians. And I knew we'd lost him: just as, earlier, I'd lost my man in the Church Street.

Tanner came back, panting. 'I'm afraid he's away!'

'Have that phone box sealed and checked for dabs.'

115

'Yes, sir. And we've got the call taped. I'll get the tape round to Liddle straight away.'

'Put another tape on.'

'Sir?'

'When he's got his breath back, we're going to hear from him again. He talked of grassing on an old mate, but then decided it was time for him to leave.'

'Did he, sir!' Tanner's eye glinted. 'Then we may not need Saxby's help after all. An old mate, sir?'

'Those were his words.'

'Yes, I like it, sir,' Tanner said. 'I like it!'

8

I left matters in Tanner's capable hands: it was high time for me to show myself to Gabrielle. Though on the phone she had been cheerful and supportive, still she had been left alone for too long. She had had visitors, I knew; Julia Mannering had called around, for one. But now it was dark again, dark in Lime Walk, dark where a pale spot lingered on the pavement; and a woman of less imagination than Gabrielle might have been forgiven for feeling moments of unease.

And truly, the situation was absurd – I was going home, but to the scene of the crime! Not, as always before, with the office door slammed, but towards the very point and crux of the affair. I felt a stab of anger; and not only towards the killer, who might well have a case for a defence counsel to argue. No: it was principally directed at Reydon, who had brought this business to our doorstep, to our quiet residential backwater, the *pied-à-terre* of which we had grown fond. Could Lime Walk ever be the same again? For myself . . . or for Gabrielle?

I walked there briskly from the police station, turning down Tanner's offer of transport. It was the time of evening when people were returning, when cars were being parked, their doors slammed, greetings called. Nothing different? I passed people I knew, people who stared at me, and then away. Some whose conversation fell silent, who lingered at their cars as I went by. I ignored them too. I chose the pavement along which Lampard and Mrs Reydon claimed to have gone, before me the same double ranks of parked cars, ahead, across the way, the shadow of the single tree. S.O.C.: scene of crime. How long had our man waited there, in the shadow? Had we been at home instead of at the theatre, must we not have spotted him, on our own excursion with the milk bottles? He had probably come, as he went, by the mews, which would account for the watchers down the street being unaware of his arrival; while from the tree he would have perfect vision of the porch of Lampard's house, and the inflammatory little scene that preceded Reydon's departure. Yet the knife had been in his pocket before that. Must not the reason for it have been...?

Then I noticed something that mildly surprised me: the windows in Reydon's house were lit. Furthermore the red Porsche was missing, had been replaced by a beige Rover 213S: a car I had seen earlier in the park of Reydon Contracts. Pale patch or no, the undaunted Mrs Reydon had come home. It may have been only to garage the Porsche and fetch clothes, but surely it required an unusual degree of sang-froid? For a moment I was inclined to ring her bell. Then I shrugged and passed on. Also lit were the windows of a flat of another lady of spirit: Mrs Cartwright.

At our own flat I didn't need my key; the door opened as I mounted the step. Gabrielle greeted me as she had let me go, with an embrace that lasted just a little too long.

'Julia was here all the afternoon, then she must leave to get a meal for Reg. But I have only to ring her, she says, and they will both come round to spend the evening. That is OK?'

I made a face. 'Better ring them.'

Poor Gabrielle! Her eyes were large. 'So, I am to lose you again so soon?'

'I'm afraid the telephone will ring before long.'

'Then ... in that case.' She turned away, briefly; but it was only to face me again, with a smile. 'In that case, my dear, we must hasten to the kitchen, where, all ready, a meal is waiting. You bring an appetite, perhaps?'

'I bring an appetite.'

'So I was thinking. Then bring it this way.'

I kissed her again first, then we went through to the kitchen. Soup was simmering on the stove, and plates of steak lay under the grill. She produced a bottle of red wine, which I uncorked as she poured the soup. By Gabrielle's standards, a simple meal, but one that exactly suited the occasion. And the phone kindly refused to ring as we got round those steaks, and the *pâtisseries* that followed. Coffee we took into the lounge. I lit my pipe. Then Gabrielle said:

'So – this man. You do not yet know who?'

I shook my head. 'Not yet. We have suspects who almost fit, but not quite. Perhaps one of them will before the end of the day.'

'But still – it is anybody?'

'Perhaps not quite! We have established a few guide-lines.'

'It could still be some stranger, passing out there?'

I put my pipe down. I said: 'Come here!'

When the telephone did ring, it was Julia Mannering, who promised to come round with her husband a little later. Gabrielle returned from the phone with a thoughtful look, and took her seat on the settee at a little distance from me. She said:

'This is gossip, my friend, and perhaps I should not be repeating it. But it fits what you call, the guide-lines, so it may be that you should hear it.'

'This is something Julia told you?'

'Uhuh. This afternoon she is all over me. She wishes to hear the smallest thing of what happened outside here last night. So I tell her, I am wishing to tell someone. I tell her everything I remember. And Julia, she is drinking it up – I think she is sorry she was not there too.'

'Did she know Reydon?'

'But yes. Julia knows everyone around here. And at first she is thinking, she is certain, that it is Philip Lampard who is the culprit. Was he not there? Had he not motive? Was he not watching for just such a moment? And Anthea Reydon – oh dear! She is in it with him. She will be Philip's mistress.'

'But then . . . second thoughts?'

Gabrielle nodded. 'I am telling her that, with me, Philip Lampard does not rank so highly, and that, last night, I am observing those two, and am willing to swear they are not lovers. But may they not be conspirators? Julia says. I say no, not to murder her husband. They are in shock, this is genuine, I am feeling they do not act a part. OK, Julia says, OK – and she is twisting a curl round her finger, you know? – but Philip isn't the only one on the list, there must be some other husbands around Kensington. Ha? I say. Get on, she says, if it had a skirt and moved Stanley was after it. He was after me. If Reg knew everything, he might be in the running too. – You mean? – She gives me a look. Don't let your imagination run away with you! No, he didn't get to first base. But it wasn't for want of trying.'

'Did Julia mention names?'

'Only one. It is only this one she is sure of. But there are others, she says, and you should ask Anthea, she is certain that Anthea knew what was going on.'

'What name did she mention?'

'One that will surprise you. It was the Forsters in Holland Park Road.'

Gabrielle was right: it did surprise me. The Forsters were

a couple we had met at Bertie's – he, a strong, silent type, a director in a financial services firm, she a quietly dressed brunette, who hovered about him like a shadow. Apparently, as with Lampard, a business deal had begun their acquaintance with Reydon: an acquaintance that had ended in a scuffle outside a hotel, and a weeping wife led away to a taxi.

'How long ago was this?'

'In the spring, Julia says. It is perhaps too long ago, yes? But there will be others, it may be quite recent, which is why I tell you this gossip.'

'Would Julia have spoken of Sara Lampard?'

'Ha – yes! They were well matched, she said, Sara and Stanley.'

'Did she mention any men in that connection?'

Gabrielle thought, but shook her head.

I drank my coffee, and just for a moment let my mind play round Alex Forster – height, age, build, colour about right, and a nose that might have struck Wilfred Liddle. A quiet, almost sulky man: one could believe in him harbouring resentments. And a wife who apparently worshipped him ... or had that been a post-Reydon development? Then the phone rang, and I dismissed him. This time the caller was Tanner. He said:

'No luck with dabs in the phone box, sir. All we got there were smears. But Liddle goes for the voice on the tape, he's ready to swear it's the same bloke.'

I told him I would be right along. Gabrielle had accompanied me into the hall. I placed my hands on her shoulders, said:

'If you would rather ... I'm sure there's a room going spare at Bertie's.'

She was about to reply indignantly, but just then a car pulled in at our frontage: the Mannerings had arrived. I lingered only to welcome them, then pressed Gabrielle's hand for an instant. And went.

I didn't go far.

Lights were still showing in the windows of the Reydon house, and after brief consideration, I mounted the steps and pressed the bell. I heard voices, then silence; then heavy footsteps approaching the door. Finally it opened a few cautious inches, to reveal the face of Arthur Hicks.

'Oh . . . it's you, is it?'

'Who were you expecting?'

'Well – no one, if you put it like that! It's just that after what happened out here . . .'

'I was hoping for a word with Mrs Reydon.'

At which point, the lady herself appeared. She didn't seem overly pleased to see me, stood staring down at me scathingly from the superior footing of the hall. She said:

'What's this then – some fresh persecution?'

'If we might go inside, Mrs Reydon?'

For a moment she stared a flat refusal, then jerked her head and stood aside for me to enter. Hicks closed the door behind us. She led the way to a room in which there were signs of some disorder. It had probably been Reydon's study, and was furnished largely with a desk, twin filing cabinets, and a safe. Drawers were pulled open, the safe door gaped, and files lay scattered on the desk and on chairs. Mrs Reydon gestured towards the confusion.

'As you can see, we are rather busy! And, before your suspicious mind goes to work, yes, I have full authority from my solicitors. So now. What can I do for you?'

I glanced at Hicks. 'This could be confidential.'

'Oh, indeed. But don't let that worry you. If it's to do with Stanley's women, you will scarcely shock Arthur. Is that your angle?'

122

I said: 'We have, of course, to pursue every line in our investigation. And it does appear that Mr Lampard was not the only disgruntled husband.'

'In fact, you have raked up some fresh scandal?'

'Another name has been mentioned.'

'Only one?'

'It has also been suggested that you could be helpful in identifying others.'

'No doubt I could. But what then?'

'I think you know the answer, Mrs Reydon. If you wish the killer of your husband to be caught, you will not be reluctant with your information.'

She stared at me waspishly, then at Hicks, who was hovering uncomfortably by the door. 'But this is absurd – quite absurd! The people you speak of can have nothing to do with it.'

I said: 'They are people with a credible motive, and such people we cannot overlook.'

'But they are known to me. They are civilized people. And in this day and age it's too ridiculous. A black eye was all they ever gave Stanley – they wouldn't have dreamed of going after him with a knife.'

I said: 'Just one amongst them.'

She tossed her head. 'I won't believe it! And I'm not going to start naming names because of a theory so preposterous. Oh no. Ask Arthur. If you want a motive, start looking here. There must be plenty of men who Stanley did the dirty on, and perhaps ruined altogether.'

I said: 'Men who you will name?'

'If you like! But Arthur can tell you better than me. He's been at the sharp end in the business, while I'm only just picking up the reins.'

We both looked at Hicks. Hicks wriggled his shoulders. He said: 'I don't know what to say, Anthea! No doubt

123

there's been some clients who've gone under, but it wouldn't be fair to drag them into this.'

'But it could have been one of them.'

'I don't know . . .'

'Yes! What was the name of that fellow you told me of – the one who went under because of the contract you landed for Phil?'

'But him . . . he's long gone.'

'Price – yes, that was the name. Price.' She turned to me. 'He was a man who supplied the borough before Phil, and when he lost the contract it finished him. So there's a name for you – Price, and there are certain to be some others. And they are the people you should be chasing, not the poor devils who Stanley cuckolded.'

I looked at Hicks, who shuffled his feet. He said: 'Of course, there could be something in it . . .'

I said: 'Are there any others who come to mind?'

'There was a fellow at Staines. But that was last year.'

'Nothing more recent?'

'Only Price. And all that happened around Easter. If he'd had a mind to do a job like this, you'd have thought he would have been on the ball sooner.'

'Where is he now?'

Hicks shook his head. 'There's quite a few round here who would like to know that! He left debts left and right, and the building society reclaimed his house.'

'Had he a wife?'

'She had to clear out too. Price had left her without a penny.'

'Do we have his description?'

'I never met him,' Hicks said. 'For me, he was just a name on a piece of paper.'

Anthea Reydon snorted. 'So there you have it,' she said. 'That's the sort of creature you should be looking for – one with a record like that. Who, literally, had his knife into Stanley. Do you still want me to rake up past scandals?'

I saw Hicks flinch. I said: 'In confidence, I would have liked those names, Mrs Reydon. But nobody can compel you. And no doubt there will be other sources.'

She glared at me. 'No doubt.'

I said: 'In the mean time, perhaps you should consider your position. It can do you no harm to assist the police in catching the man who so brutally made away with your husband.'

Her eyes blazed. 'Just get out! Arthur, see this gentleman to the door.'

'But Anthea . . . !'

'See him out – and make sure you bolt the door after him!'

The unhappy Hicks followed me to the door, and hastened obsequiously to open it. As we parted, he murmured:

'She's like that, squire . . . she's under stress. Don't pay too much attention to it!'

So what had been the provocation behind that killing – was it sex, business, or simple callous behaviour? I pondered it through the streets on my way back to the police station, but neither logic nor intuition offered a lead to the conundrum. Sex had been vibrant in that final scene, but financial interest had not been absent, while somewhere close – and perhaps closer than we knew – had hovered the unstable element of hatred. And, behind all this, the Voice . . . which of the three motives was represented there? As I walked, I kept my eyes switching about me. But no shadowy figure lurked to vanish into some convenient alley-way.

'Has the tail on Saxby reported?'

I found Tanner chewing a thoughtful sandwich in his

125

office. He half rose as I entered, then settled back on his chair with a grin.

'Yes, sir, half an hour ago. Saxby went home like a good little boy. But it seems it was only to change his clobber. Cressy says now, he looks almost respectable.'

'So he's on the wander again?'

'Right. But he's got Cressy hard on his heels.'

'Did Cresswell report any sightings?'

'Nothing yet, sir. I'd say our little friend has gone to ground.'

'What about Salmon?'

Tanner gave me a wink. 'It gets better all the time, sir! Now we know that dear Donna was in the Bunch of Grapes till closing.'

I related my interview with Mrs Reydon, and at the mention of Price's name, Tanner stopped chewing. But then, after a draught of coffee, he reluctantly shook his head.

'It's a nice idea, sir, very nice. If only all this had happened eight months ago. But we haven't seen Joe Price in these parts since he cleaned out his account and took a powder.'

'You can be sure of that.'

'He's on our books, sir. The County Court has got business with him. He's up to here with half the tradesmen, not to mention the allowance for his wife and kids.'

'Where is she now?'

'Gone back to her parents – over Kensal Green way I think she is. The house was repossessed, and he only had his yard on a lease.'

'So Reydon busted him good and proper.'

'Only that was eight months ago, sir.'

'Would he fit the description?'

'Reckon he might. But I never had any close dealings with him myself.'

I said: 'It might just be worth while to get a line on him.'

Tanner grimaced. 'We've been trying for ever. But I'll put it about that it's for the big time, and that way we may get a grass.'

The phone went. Tanner laid down a sandwich. He listened for a moment with pondering eyes. Then he lowered the phone, said:

'It's Cressy, sir. And it sounds like Saxby's been having a ball!'

I took the phone. 'Cresswell?'

'I'm ringing from the Cat and Fiddle, sir. I've got Saxby here under close surveillance. I've just had to separate him and Salmon.'

'You mean they've been fighting?'

'A bit of a barney, sir. Saxby's been round to Bloemfontein Road. He started bawling outside Salmon's house, and Salmon came out, and there was a ruckus. He was accusing Salmon of doing for Reydon, and then trying to blame it on him. Salmon said he was crazy as a coot, and that it must have been him who did it. That's when it got exciting, sir, and I had to step in and separate them. Salmon went back in, and I brought Saxby along here. He's quietened off now, sir, but he's really got it in for Salmon. Do I bring him in?'

I said: 'Yes . . . I think so. Will you be needing any assistance?'

'No thanks, sir. I can manage him.'

'Then bring him in straight away.'

I laid the phone down. Tanner's eyes gleamed at me. He said:

'That silly sod! He knows something.'

'Something,' I said. 'About Salmon.'

'Yeah,' Tanner said. 'Yeah.' And he grabbed a fresh sandwich.

If Saxby did not yet look wholly respectable, still, his appearance had substantially improved. A well-cut tweed coat, which had an aura of both-balls, replaced the former threadbare relic. He had changed his trousers and his shoes, and now wore a passable pork-pie hat; all that was really letting him down was his collar-length hair and his bristly chin.

His manner had changed also: there was no vagueness now in the pale brown eyes. He stalked into the office almost impatiently, and made straight for the chair placed for him. One further modification was a dull bruise on the side of his jaw, while a certain rawness of knuckle was apparent in the hands which he placed on his knees. I looked him over for a moment, then said:

'I hear you've been in some trouble, Saxby.'

'It wasn't my fault!' He jerked in the chair. 'But of course, you're going to blame me, aren't you?'

'Wasn't it you who started it?'

'No, it wasn't. I merely wanted to tell the brute that I knew.'

'You went round to his house, and created a nuisance?'

'But that was simply to get him out there.'

'And – when you got him out there?'

'All right! I'm sure you'll believe him, and not me.'

'Didn't you utter certain accusations?'

'It's true – everything I said there was true.' Saxby's hands grappled together. 'It was him who put you on to me, wasn't it? You told me someone tipped you off, and there was no one else who could have done it.'

'You thought it was Salmon?'

'I know it was him. He's always had it in for me. And now this thing – he knew. He knew I wouldn't have a leg to stand on.'

'How would he know?'

'He . . . just knew. And you, you're going to believe him,

aren't you? I've got everything against me, he knew that. It's too cruel!'

I said: 'And you? You're blaming him?'

'Yes, because why else would he be doing it? He didn't have to go tipping you off, and there can only be one reason.'

'That Salmon is guilty?'

'Yes.'

I stared, and slowly shook my head.

'But it has to be that. It has to be.'

I kept staring at him. 'No.'

'Please – yes!'

'No.'

He sat gazing, sweating, his hands working on his lap. Some of the old vagueness was back in his eyes, the help-lessness in his expression. Then his gaze, his head, sank. I said:

'You have a better reason for accusing Salmon, haven't you?'

'I don't need –'

'Look at me, Saxby!' He dragged his eyes back to mine. I said: 'Now listen carefully. If we find you know something which you have refused to tell us, we can charge you with obstruction, and perhaps even with complicity after the event. Do you understand?'

'Yes, but you'll only think –!'

'So have you something to tell us?'

'No! I –'

'Have you?'

His eyes held to mine desperately. At last he gave a little gasp, and in a whisper said:

'He . . . he was there.'

'Salmon was there?'

'Yes . . .'

'In Lime Walk?'

He could only nod.

'So then you were there too?'

'Yes. But . . . I didn't kill Mr Reydon.'

I said: 'Let's get this clear. You say that you and Salmon were in Lime Walk?'

'No, not then . . . it was later. After the police car went in . . .'

'It was later?'

'When I was in Lime Walk! I didn't go there till all the fuss . . .'

'And it was then you saw Salmon there?'

'No . . . before. You don't understand!'

'What don't I understand?'

'You see, I saw him – and I know he saw me! But he wanted to pretend he didn't, he wouldn't look. He was across the street . . .'

'In Lime Walk?'

'No. This was earlier . . . I was in the Church Street when I saw him. He was walking fast, with his head down, as though he didn't want anyone to recognize him. He was wearing an old coat and a cap pulled low, but I knew it was him as soon as I saw him. And he saw me, but he wouldn't look, just kept his head down and walked on. It seemed so odd. I kept watching him. And he turned off into Lime Walk.'

I kept my eyes tight on his. 'You're sure of this?'

'Yes . . . oh, I know you're not going to believe me!'

'At what time was this?'

'About half-past ten . . . just before . . .'

'And what were you doing around there at that time?'

'I told you, I couldn't stand being indoors alone.'

'By pure chance, you were in the vicinity of Lime Walk?'

'But it wasn't me! I didn't kill him.'

Still I held his eyes. 'Carry on.'

'It was after that . . . I hadn't gone far . . .'

'You didn't follow Salmon into Lime Walk?'

'No! I was never there till afterwards.'

'So?'

'So this police car came by, didn't it? It had got its siren going. And I saw it take the turn towards Lime Walk, and at once I remembered seeing Salmon. I thought . . . I don't know what! But he'd been behaving so oddly. And I did wonder . . . I knew that Mr Reydon had moved there.'

'And you followed the car?'

'No, not at once. But then some other police cars went in there. So then I did, and I saw all the people . . . at first, I thought the body must have been Salmon's.'

'Who told you it wasn't?'

'I – I could see it. And Mrs Reydon. And Mr Lampard.'

'You didn't see Salmon?'

'No, of course not! But I knew . . . I mean, who else?'

I said: 'You had this important information, but it didn't occur to you to come forward?'

He shrank a little from me. 'I couldn't very well, could I?'

'Why not?'

'Because . . . I mean! I had to get away before I was recognized.'

'You anticipated suspicion?'

He shrank further. 'Haven't you been after me . . . all the time?'

I stared, and shook my head. 'So you took off. What exactly did you intend to do then?'

Saxby pulled on his clamped hands. 'I don't know. Perhaps . . . it could have been the river.'

I glanced at Tanner's intrigued face: Tanner shook his head. 'No questions, sir!'

'Right,' I said. 'Take Mr Saxby along to write us a fresh statement.'

'But . . . !'

'Just what you've been telling us, Mr Saxby.'

He stared at me with wretched eyes. Then Cresswell tapped him on the shoulder, and he got shakily to his feet and was led out. When the door closed, Tanner gave a long sigh.

'So now we've got it, sir – we've got the goods!'

I said: 'Almost, but not quite. We can't nail Salmon to the knife.'

'It'll come, sir. It must come. It could be that Salmon was faking his voice. It could have fooled Liddle, sounded close enough to that joker on the phone.'

I shrugged. 'It's possible.'

'I'd say odds on, sir. So do we send a car to Bloemfontein Road?'

I said: 'Two cars, and also a search warrant. Because Salmon wasn't wearing his Sunday coat last night.'

'No more he was, sir!' Tanner's eyes were dancing. 'And there could be a spot of blood on the sleeve. And then we would have him nailed to the knife, whether Liddle goes for him or not.'

'So put it in motion.'

'Leave it to me, sir!'

Tanner went charging out of the office. I lit a cogitative pipe. Had we really got this case licked at last? It was adding up. Salmon, by a short head, had always been our leading contender, and now we had him placed at the scene . . . if not as yet with the knife in his hand. A man with a motive, perhaps a double motive. A man whose physique and whose garb fitted. A pity that Liddle had turned him down, but as Tanner said, that might be explicable.

Tanner returned. 'All in hand, sir. But we've got two visitors who're asking for a word with you. They say it's important, only I wasn't sure if you'd want to be interrupted just now.'

132

'Who are they?'

'Lampard and Mrs Reydon.'

I stared. 'And they say it's important?'

'Seem all steamed up about something, sir.'

'In that case, you'd better wheel them in.'

9

'I've been telling Philip what I told you – and Philip wasn't quite so contemptuously dismissive! If you would listen to the people who understand this business, you might be a little closer to arresting the culprit.'

'I regret that I am rather busy, Mrs Reydon –'

'You see? Already you're trying to brush us aside! The facts don't matter. You've made up your mind, and nothing that we say is of the slightest consequence.'

'If it relates to your husband's infidelities –'

'Didn't I tell you?' She threw a triumphant look at her companion. 'That's all that counts with him – Stanley's women. He wants to hear of nothing else but about them.'

She had stalked in towing Lampard behind her, and now stood furiously in front of the desk. Lampard was looking rather less assured; he stood by with a sullen expression on his flushed face. I said:

'I really am busy, Mrs Reydon. But if you have something relevant to tell me –'

'Otherwise, do you think I'd be wasting my time here, when I have so many other things to attend to?'

'Then, if you will sit down?'

'Oh, thank you so much.'

But she paused before accepting the chair that Tanner placed for her. Lampard pulled one up for himself, a little to one side, and sat himself cautiously.

'Now Philip – you tell him.'

'Anthea, I'm not sure –'

'Just tell him, Philip! Me, he'll probably suspect of having made it up.'

Lampard looked as though he feared a similar fate, but he fixed his eyes on me determinedly. He said: 'It's about the man who Anthea mentioned to you, Joseph Price. We may have seen him last night.'

'Joseph Price . . . ?'

'The man who went bust. Who lost out when Stanley fixed me that contract. I didn't know it was going to break him, of course. He was a man I'd done business with a few times.'

'So you'd met him personally?'

'Once or twice. He had his yard in Earls Court. I'd give him a ring when I was short of something, and once I was able to supply him with timber. Well, the deals with the borough were his life-line, and when he lost them he was through. I only found out when I rang his yard and found I was talking to a used car lot.'

'And – you say you saw him last night?'

'Oh, I know we should have told you before! But it wasn't until Anthea mentioned the name to me that I realized who it might have been that we saw. And then I got thinking. Because if Stanley had really hurt someone, then that someone was Joseph Price.'

'Of course it was!' Mrs Reydon exclaimed. 'All this business about women is nonsense. People don't kill for such reasons these days, it has to be someone who had really been hurt.'

I said: 'So let's hear what you can tell me.'

'Well – we saw him. Philip saw him.'

'Perhaps you can enlarge on that?'

She turned on Lampard. 'Tell him, Philip!'

Frowningly, Lampard said: 'I can't swear to it, but it was

after everything got quiet in the Walk. I daresay it was half after ten or later, and we saw this fellow come slinking by. He didn't see us. He was on the other pavement. He kept pausing by cars and squinting around. I suspected him of being a car thief, and I said as much to Anthea.'

'Yes, that's just what he looked like,' Mrs Reydon said. 'Though we didn't actually see him try the handles of any cars. But there was something sneaky and underhand about him, and he was certainly keeping a look-out.'

'And . . . you thought you knew him?'

'No, not quite that,' Lampard frowned. 'But there was something about him, something familiar. About his figure. The way he moved. Then, when Anthea mentioned Price, it struck me, that the fellow could well have been him. As I say, I can't swear to it, but we thought we ought to pass it on.'

'Did you see where he went?'

'We lost sight of him. But he was going in the right direction. Soon after that a car went up the Walk, only there was no sign of him then.'

'Can you describe him?'

Lampard shook his head. 'He was never close enough for that. Just that he was a big fellow, like Price, and wearing something dark. And a hat.'

'In fact, he could have been the man you saw later?'

'Of course he could!' Mrs Reydon said. 'Philip pretends he can't be certain, but I can. It was the same man.'

Lampard shook his head again. 'We only saw his back,' he said. 'And he was away in a couple of shakes. It could have been, probably was him, but honestly I couldn't take my oath on it.'

'Oh, Philip – who else could it have been?'

But Lampard wasn't going to be persuaded. He said: 'It was all over so quickly, and then there were cars between them and us.'

After a pause, I said: 'Then perhaps you can describe Price?'

'I'll have a shot,' Lampard said. 'He's about forty-five, tallish, powerful, moves around like a cat.'

'Colouring?'

'Fairish.'

'Features?'

His frown came back. 'How would you describe them? It's the sort of face that makes you look twice . . . craggy, is the only word I can think of.'

'A prominent nose?'

Lampard nodded. 'And deep lines down each side of his face. And greyish skin, rough-looking. And a chin that juts out.'

'What about his voice?'

'A sort of growl. He's an odd sort of cove altogether.'

I said: 'Would you remember that voice again?'

Lampard looked cautious. 'I suppose I might.'

I nodded to Tanner, who fetched the tape that Liddle had found so convincing. We played it, then replayed it: but the result was disappointing. At the end of the performance, Lampard shook his head.

'I can't be sure of that, either.'

'But – it could be him?'

'Yes, it could – if he had the father and mother of sore throats! Is it important?'

I shrugged. I said: 'Thank you for coming to us, Mr Lampard. I shall, of course, require a written statement, both from yourself and Mrs Reydon.'

'And you're going to round him up?' Mrs Reydon demanded. 'No more of this rubbish about Stanley and his women?'

'We shall certainly hope to talk to Price, Mrs Reydon.'

'And that's all we're to get for our trouble in coming here!'

137

She stalked out as she had entered, with the tight-faced Lampard following in her wake. They almost ran into an incoming Edith, who carried a bundle of some sort in his arms. He dumped it on a chair.

'Look at this, sir! We found it hidden away in Salmon's garage.'

He unfolded a grimy, oil-stained black coat, and wrapped up in it a dingy black cap. Tanner fell on it. He spread it out. He stood gazing lovingly at the coat, the cap. He said:

'Bugger Joe Price, sir! Now we've got Salmon where we want him.'

There were no obvious blood-spots on the sleeves, but that was a job for forensic anyway. What we had in the coat was confirmation of the testimony Saxby had given us, and of the presumption that Salmon was the man seen later in Lime Walk by Lampard and Mrs Reydon. We left it spread on the chair for Salmon to see when he came in. We also had Mary and her pad squatting at the end of the desk. And this time there was certainly less bounce about Salmon when Edith ushered him into the office.

'Sit yourself, Salmon.'

His eyes had gone to the coat, then at once he'd jerked them away. He sat. His eyes momentarily met mine, then fell to the desk. His mouth was bitter.

'I suppose you know why you've been brought back here, Salmon?'

'No, I bloody well don't! You've got a nerve.'

'You think we should be satisfied with your account of last night?'

'I don't give a damn if you are or you aren't.'

'You have nothing to add to it?'

'Why should I have?'

138

I said: 'Think carefully, Salmon. We haven't been idle. If there is anything you ought to tell us, it might be best if you were to tell us now.'

'You go to hell.'

'For example, if you weren't where you said you were last night.'

'Only I was. You ask Donna. I was never out of her sight all evening.'

I said: 'Then you were drinking in the Cat and Fiddle?'

'Sod the Cat and Fiddle!'

'But that's where Donna was last night.'

'Oh shit.' His mouth twisted. 'If she was, then she'd only nipped out for a quick one.'

'Which lasted till closing?'

'I can't help that. She was in and out, but I was there. I may have dropped off, and never missed her, but that's all about that. I was there.'

'At nine. At ten?'

'Bloody yes.'

'At ten thirty?'

'Yes!'

'And after that?'

He stared at the desk, his eyes small, his mouth shut tight.

I said: 'Why was that coat hidden in your garage?'

'Who says it was hidden? I just keep it there.'

'You keep a coat in the garage?'

'Yes, I bloody do. For mucking with the car. It's cold in there.'

'You work on your car in a coat?'

'Why shouldn't I? Tell me that.'

'And wearing a cap?'

'Shit, why not?'

I gazed at him, and shook my head. I said: 'You were wearing that coat and cap last night. But you weren't working on your car then. Nor were you watching television. Nor sitting asleep in your chair. Where were you, Salmon?'

'I was where I said!'

'At nine? At ten?'

His eyes were ugly.

'At ten thirty?'

His mouth was working.

'And after that?'

'You bloody sod!'

'Well?'

'I could do for you. And I could do for that bloody wimp Saxby. Oh yes, I saw him there. And the bastard has grassed on me, hasn't he?'

'You saw him where?'

'Didn't he tell you?'

'I'm asking you to tell me, Salmon.'

'It could have been him, have you thought of that?'

I stared, and nodded. 'You were both there.'

'So what was he doing there?'

'What I wish to know is what you were doing there.'

Salmon was scowling at me aggressively, at the same time shiftily, almost with a measure of calculation.

'Me! I was minding my business, wasn't I? Could be I was looking for a tart. A bloke can go for a stroll of an evening without him sticking a knife into someone.'

'But at that place. At that time?'

'You're telling me, mate. I'm admitting nothing. If you want to take the word of a drip like Saxby, that's your affair, not mine.'

'Yet . . . you saw Saxby there?'

'That could have been any time.'

'As you were proceeding along the Church Street?'

'If you say so.'

'Dressed in that coat and that cap?'

'Why not?'

'Prior', I said, 'to your entering Lime Walk, where two independent witnesses place you, and proceeding in the direction of Mr Reydon's house, perhaps twenty-five minutes before Mr Reydon was stabbed?'

'You . . . bastard!' His eyes jumped at me. 'I was never in Lime Walk – never!'

'Described as proceeding furtively, along the left-hand pavement, and hiding from the lights of a passing car.'

He jumped to his feet, was thrust down again by Edith. He sat panting and staring hatred at me. He gabbled: 'You're going to do me for this – you're going to do me, aren't you? And I was bloody miles from Lime Walk by then.'

'Then you admit being there.'

'No, I sodding wasn't.'

'At the place. At the time. And, of course, with a motive.'

'I'll kill you, you sod!'

'And answering the killer's description – same build, same colouring, same clothing.'

'I'll kill you!'

I said: 'Before we go any further, I am going to issue a warning, Salmon. You don't have to answer questions, but if you do your answers will be taken down and may be given in evidence. Is that clear?'

Only too clear! This time he was off the chair and sending Edith reeling. He made for the door, but before he could reach it, Tanner had taken him in a rugby tackle. They crashed to the floor. Edith joined in. For a moment, it was all they could do to hold him. Poor Mary, wide-eyed, crouched close to the desk, pad and pencil fallen from her hand. Finally the swearing Salmon was pinioned, dragged back and slammed down on the chair. Still he struggled,

141

with the determined Edith maintaining a stranglehold on his neck. Tanner panted:

'Do I shackle this beauty?'

'You sods, you can't do it to me!' Salmon gasped.

I said: 'What's it to be, Salmon?'

'I never did it!'

'Do you behave, or do we have to use handcuffs?'

'I tell you I never –!'

But Edith was nearly choking him. In the end he subsided, gasping, on the chair. Reluctantly, Edith relaxed his hold, but stood close behind Salmon, alert to renew it. And Mary recovered her pad from the floor, and scribbled down the warning I had just delivered. I said:

'That was foolish, Salmon. You're never going to run away from this. So either you tell us the truth about last night, or leave us to draw our own conclusions. Which is it to be?'

'I didn't kill the bugger!'

'But you were present in Lime Walk last night.'

'No – I mean, not then. I wasn't there when someone shoved a knife in him.'

'Between half-past ten and eleven you were there.'

'I tell you, I effed off before it happened.'

'But you were there.'

'So I bloody was!'

'Then if it wasn't for that purpose, why were you there?'

'I tell you –!'

'Yes?'

His eyes slanted from mine. 'It was that blonde bit. Lampard's missus. She'd given me the come-on once or twice. I couldn't see any harm in giving it a go.'

'You were there to visit Mrs Lampard?'

'Yes, I'm telling you! Only I could see she'd got someone else there. So I just pissed off, didn't I? That's the only reason I was there.'

142

'You went up the Walk?'

'I pissed off!'

'In the direction of Mr Reydon's house?'

He stared at the desk.

I said: 'From where you would have to watch Mrs Lampard's loving farewell of Mr Reydon?'

'Oh, you sod!' Salmon swore.

'You did see it, didn't you?' I said. 'The woman you fancied embracing and kissing the man for whom already you had sufficient hatred?'

'You bastard, I didn't wait to see that!'

'And then, the unsuspecting Mr Reydon's return?'

'I wasn't there!'

'Till he turned, with his back to you. As you waited. In the shadow of the tree.'

It happened again: he tried to spring from the chair, but this time both Edith and Tanner were on top of him. He was jammed down again promptly, with Edith's arm crooked round his throat. 'There, there, my little man!' Tanner chided. 'You'll upset the lady, carrying on like that.'

'You bastards, you bastards!' Salmon gasped. 'You're going to have me for this one, aren't you? I knew it as soon as I walked in here.'

'As though we would,' Tanner smirked. 'And you with your neck stuck out from here to eternity.'

'But I never killed him!'

'Tell the man,' Tanner said. 'Me, you're going to have bursting into tears.'

I waited till Edith had released him again, then I said: 'It all adds up, Salmon. Have it which way you like, but everything we know is pointing at you.'

'But I didn't kill him. You've got to believe me!'

'We shall, of course, take note of what you say.'

'But I was never there – I'd cleared out! It wasn't what you think at all.'

'Then what was it?'

'Do I have to tell you?'

I stared and said nothing.

'Oh, bloody shit!' He looked away, looked at the coat, looked at nothing. He said: 'If you must know . . . I was up the Walk to nick a car.'

'To – steal a car.'

'Aren't I telling you?' His eyes were fixed on me in desperation. 'I've got a bloody wife and kids and a mortgage, and Reydon slung me out in the gutter. You have to do something. And there aren't any jobs. And I knew where I could flog a hot one. So there you are, that's how it was. I was up the Walk to knock off a car.'

'And – you stole one?'

'Yes, but not there! And you've bloody well got to believe me. As soon as I stepped into the frigging Walk I could feel that someone's eyes were on me. There was a couple in a car, no doubt you're on to them, and an old biddy putting a cat out. Then this car came cruising by, like it might have been the filth doing a recce. I didn't like it, so I scapa'd. And I was never there when Reydon bought it.'

'You weren't there.'

'No! I went out the back way, worked round to Holland Park Road.'

'And stole a car?'

'Like it was waiting for me, with the key still in the ignition. I watched it pull up. The bloke had got his hands full, a briefcase, coat and a couple of bags. He went on in, and as soon as the door closed I nipped into the car and was on my way.'

'What make of car?'

'An XR2.'

'And you disposed of it where?'

144

'Do I have to tell you that?'

Tanner said softly: 'Oh, I think you should. With so many going missing round these parts lately.'

Salmon gave him an ugly look. 'Oh the hell with it then! If you must know, it was Ikey Fischer. I drove it straight round to his last night, and this morning he tipped me a measly five hundred.'

'Ikey Fischer,' Tanner said. 'Well, well! The boys at the Court will like to know that. Edith, fetch me the stolen-car list.'

The list was fetched; Tanner ran his eye down it. Then, sighing, he handed the list to me. The last item recorded was a '91 XR2, stolen from outside an address in Holland Park Road. And the time of the theft was recorded: approximately 11.05 on the previous evening.

'Sad, isn't it, sir?' Tanner murmured. 'But he'd have had to run like the clappers.'

I shrugged and stared at the scowling Salmon, whom the record was so incisively loosening from our clutches. I said:

'All right then, Salmon! For the moment we are prepared to accept that story. But the fact remains that you were on the spot at or about the time of the crime. If you saw anything, can tell us anything, it might help you on another occasion. Almost certainly you would have passed within yards, perhaps within feet, of the murderer. What have you to say?'

'You mean – you'll drop charges about the car?'

I shook my head. 'I didn't say that.'

'Then you know what you can do, don't you?'

I said: 'Think about it, Salmon.'

He went on scowling. He said: 'I didn't see a bleeding thing. Just that couple in the car and the old biddy with her cat. Then that car that went by. It stopped higher up and dropped someone off. So then I'd had enough of sodding Lime Walk, and I slung my hook up the alley.'

'Did you see who it was the car dropped off?'

'A bloke, a bird. I dunno.'

'Would you have passed anyone in the alley?'

Salmon paused for an instant, staring. 'You mean up by the garages – up there?'

'Anyone at all in that area.'

'Well – yeah. I did see a bloke. I thought he was on the same game as myself.'

'Can you describe him?'

'He looked a rough bugger. When he saw me he pulled into a gateway. But I didn't want any truck with him, any more than he did with me.'

'How was he dressed?'

'Now you're asking. He was all bundled up in a coat and titfer. A big bloke, big as me. Looked like he'd been on the streets a while.'

'And you saw him by the garages?'

'Hanging about there.'

I glanced at Mary. 'Have you got that down?' Mary nodded. I said: 'We shall need a statement from you, Salmon. You may have given us important information.'

'Here!' Salmon glared at me. 'I'm not signing any bloody confession.'

'So just your account of meeting this man.'

'But what about the other?'

I said: 'The other you can safely leave with us.'

Salmon was removed. I ordered coffee. For a while, we sat silently drinking it. Just briefly, in that office, we had seemed to have the Reydon case sewn up. And now, we hadn't. We were back with the unknown, a voice on the phone, an anonymous figure: all still to do. And only one prospect that might or might not have some connection. I sighed, and lit my pipe. Too often, that was the way things went!

Tanner said: 'So what now, sir?'

I said: 'We'll have to step up the hunt for Price. We know now it wasn't him who Lampard saw in the Walk, but it could still have been him behind the knife.'

'The bloke Salmon saw.'

I nodded. 'Salmon almost certainly ran into the killer. And if it wasn't Price, we need to know that, keep an open mind for other angles.'

Tanner said: 'A funny thing about Ikey Fischer! I suppose it's nothing to do with this business, sir. But it's on Price's old yard that Ikey runs his dodgy car lot.'

'That was Price's old yard?'

'Right, sir.' Tanner wrinkled his brow. 'I don't suppose . . .'

I shrugged. 'Price is holed up somewhere! The yard might be a good place to start looking.'

'Well, it's handy, sir. I think I'll give the boys in the Court a little ring.'

He rang them. I smoked. Till now, I hadn't given Price my close attention. Yet there could be no question that, as Mrs Reydon claimed, he had suffered a grievous, a calamitous injury. Because of Reydon's manoeuvres he had been reduced from a man of substance to a hunted fugitive, had lost his home, lost his family, and by now was probably on his uppers. Motive enough, surely! Yet the catastrophe had happened way back at Easter. Could the revenge have simmered with him so long, through summer, through autumn, till hard on Christmas?

Tanner hung up. 'They're on to it, sir! If Price is holed up there, we'll have him. One of the boys there knows him by sight, and he owes a few debts round the Court too. I'm beginning to like him.'

I said: 'It's early days, yet.'

147

'But he does fit the picture,' Tanner said.

'So did Salmon. And Saxby.'

'But them we've ruled out, sir,' Tanner said.

The phone went. He snatched it up. I saw his eyes go suddenly still. Slowly, he passed the phone over, and I held it to my ear.

'Gently here.'

This time, there wasn't any background of traffic. The voice said: 'The bloke you want is Sam Mason, and this one is for real.'

I said: 'Sam Mason?' – and I heard Tanner catch his breath.

The voice said: 'You've got it. He was after Reydon for his wallet.'

'He mugged Reydon?'

'Right. Now I'll tell you where to find him. Flat 33, Hot-black Court. That's on Ogden Street in the Bush.'

'Would you repeat that?'

But the voice was gone. Hurriedly, I dropped the phone and scribbled the address. Then I looked enquiringly at Tanner, who was staring open-eyed.

'A Sam Mason – do we know him?'

'You bet your life we know him, sir! Three years for mugging a milkman, and he was carrying a knife that time, too.'

'Would he fit the description?'

'Not far off. And here's the comic bit, sir. When we did him for the milkman, he was working for our friend Joe Price.'

'For Joe Price . . .'

'Yes, sir.'

'Then let's get a car round there – quick!'

10

In fact the patrol car beat us to it by only a matter of minutes. Ogden Street was council-land, and Hotblack Court its sleaziest establishment. We parked among wrecks of ancient cars and chased up a stairway where even the graffiti seemed to have lost heart. Youths, blacks, hung around watching, but every door was tight shut. 33 was on the first-floor gallery. We came on the two patrolmen beating on the door. And there was another smell hanging about that gallery besides that of stale urine and boiled cabbage: the smell of gas.

'He doesn't answer, sir!'

'Break it down.'

There wasn't time for subtleties. One after the other, the two patrolmen launched themselves against the stubborn door. It crashed open.

'Holy Moses –!'

Gas billowed out from the unlit interior. One of the patrolmen reached for the light-switch, but I swept his hand aside.

'You could blow us up!'

'But if the bloke is in there –'

'Stand back and let it clear a bit.'

Luckily, we were on an open gallery. But, from the depths of the flat, one could hear a sinister hissing. After the worst of the build-up passed, I said:

'One of you put a handkerchief over your face and get in there!'

It took two attempts to find the gas-fire, and two more to locate the tap. Then it was the turn of the window, which eventually the patrolman had to smash. He came out gasping and hung on the rail. He said:

'The bloke is in there. He's on the bed. I jammed my hand into his face. It felt cold. I think he's a gonner.'

'Get an ambulance here.'

The second patrolman left at a run. At each end of the gallery figures were collecting, furtive, silent: watching. There were others down by the cars. But not a door along the gallery had opened.

'Ambulance on its way, sir.'

I sniffed at the gas. A thin, icy draught was proceeding from the flat. I gave it another five minutes by my watch: then I switched on the light, and went in.

'The poor bloody sod – do you think he knew?'

The man on the bed was still alive, just. One of the patrolmen, who'd had first-aid training, was seeking to give him artificial respiration. A man of about fifty, dressed rough, several days' growth of beard on his cheeks: coarse features, clumsy hands, height five-ten, five-eleven.

'We're sure it's Mason?'

'Yes, that's him, sir. I was wondering what happened to him when he came out. He had a missus, but she took off. They used to live in Trory Street.'

By the bed, on a chair, stood a whisky bottle, and beside it a tumbler containing dregs. The whisky bottle was almost empty; it bore the price label of a local supermarket.

'Well, it's one way to go...'

Now the gas was clearing, one could catch the fume of

150

whisky. A few drops had been spilled on the chair, and the tumbler stood awry, half-on, half-off. Tanner made to stand it straighter, but I stopped him.

'We shall need to have this place dusted.'

'Dusted . . . ? You think?'

'I think nothing – yet. But this isn't a time to take chances.'

I moved around that dismal apartment, which was little more than a bed-sit. Everywhere there were signs of poverty, of neglect, of despair. An empty wardrobe, empty cupboards, soiled underwear dumped in a corner, a couple of dirty plates in the sink, a bath used only as a receptacle for litter. And the toilet smelled, even in competition with the lingering fumes of gas. Just one surprise: in the larder, food that clearly had been bought recently – cheese, bread, eggs, tea and a bottle of long-life milk. If Mason had made an attempt at suicide, it would appear to have been a very recent decision.

A clamour below was the ambulance arriving: the crew appeared, carrying a rolled stretcher. They took a quick look at Mason, on whom our patrolman was still labouring. Then one of them shook his head.

'We'll do our best, sir. But I'm afraid he's had it.'

'Where are you taking him?'

'St Stephen's. You can enquire about him there.'

They unrolled the stretcher and loaded him. There was no sign of consciousness about Mason. A feeble, shallow breathing was all, a last faint contact with existence. They secured straps round his lolling body and carted him out: we heard the ambulance leave.

'What now, sir?'

'Get your team here right away. I'll see if I can have a word with the neighbours.'

Tanner paused, then set off to the car.

Outside, I found a door about two inches open.

I said: 'Police. I wish to talk to you.'

For a moment, the door didn't open any further. Then, very cautiously, the gap widened, to reveal an elderly black woman wearing a flowered head-scarf. Her brown eyes fixed on me anxiously. She said:

'Are you really the police, man?'

I took out my warrant and showed it her. She stared at it frowningly, then back at me. She said:

'We have to be careful around here, man, but I guess you's on the level. You ain't the rent-man, and he's the only other one who comes here in a suit. You want in?'

'If I may.'

She stepped back to allow me to enter. It was a flat identical with that next door, but very different in its appearance. The woman bolted the door behind us, then ushered me to a seat. She was a plump, motherly-looking woman, clad in a thick skirt and a knobbly jumper. I said:

'How shall I call you, ma'am?'

'I'm Phoebe Dawkins, and I ain't no ma'am.'

I said: 'This is about your neighbour, Mrs Dawkins. I regret to say he has met with a misfortune.'

'Was he the stiff they just carried off?'

'Mr Mason has been removed to hospital.'

'And it was him – the bloke what has that flat?'

'To the best of our knowledge, he is the tenant.'

Mrs Dawkins wrinkled her nose. 'Trash,' she said. 'Lousy trash. That's the sort we get round here now, no-good trash. It used to be different.'

'Were you acquainted with Mr Mason?'

'What?' She drew herself up. 'No, I wasn't, man, not with him nor any of his pals. Me, I keep myself decent. I don't mix with trash like that feller. So what happened, was he in a fight?'

I said: 'He is suffering from exposure to gas.'

'Gas.' The brown eyes were big. 'You're telling me he tried to do himself in?'

'Would that surprise you?'

She shook her head. 'Nothing would surprise me about trash like him. Half the time he was stoned, and don't ask me where he got the money for that.'

'He was a habitual drunkard.'

'You're kidding me, man. Most every day he was on the juice. You'd see him roaring and staggering by here, hardly able to get his key in the door. And now – he's done for himself?'

'It could perhaps have been an accident.'

'You mean like he was too drunk to strike a light for the gas?'

'That's one possibility.'

Mrs Dawkins gazed at me, her brown eyes imagining it. Then she said:

'But are you sure it's him?'

'Are we sure . . . ?'

'There's this bloke who's dossing with him. I've seen him pretty juiced, too. And he's the ugliest sod you ever set eyes on.'

I said: 'A man was staying with Mason?'

'He dosses there, man. He's been around here the past fortnight. Real trash he is, too, like he'd been sleeping rough for ever. Sure it wasn't him?'

I said: 'Could you describe him?'

Her eyes puckered. 'He's rough, man, rough. A big bloke with an ugly face and a bust nose. Or that's how it looks.'

'How old?'

'Looks a hundred. Mebbe put him around fifty.'

'How is he dressed?'

'A dirty old coat. And a hat pulled over his ears.'

'Have you heard his voice?'

'That's rough too, man, like he needed to have a gargle.

153

He's a bloke you wouldn't want to meet up a dark alley. So are you sure it wasn't him?'

I shook my head. 'When did you last see him?'

'That's what I mean,' Mrs Dawkins said. 'About seven o'clock I saw him go in there, with a bottle of scotch sticking out of his pocket.'

'At about seven?'

'My son was here, I was just seeing him out of the door. Then this rough bloke comes by. We both of us had a good stare at him.'

'Was Mason in at that time?'

'Opened the door for him, didn't he?'

'And you're sure about the bottle of whisky?'

'Ask my son. He saw it too.'

I said: 'And later, you wouldn't have seen this man leave?'

Mrs Dawkins looked blank. 'No, man. When my son left I bolted the door, and that's how it stayed till I heard the ambulance. But it wasn't him they took off?'

'It wasn't him.'

'That's a pity,' Mrs Dawkins said. 'They were bleeding trash, the pair of them. But he was the one I liked least.'

I went back to the flat next door, where Tanner was waiting for his team to arrive, and where one of the patrolmen stood on guard to keep those silent, slinking figures at a distance. Still the smell of gas dogged the place, along with the other sleazy odours; and the flat looked particularly dismal after Mrs Dawkins' cosy nest. I found Tanner poring over the broken-spring settee, over which was now spread a dilapidated sleeping-bag. He said:

'I found this bundled up under a cushion, sir. Do you reckon Mason could have had a lodger?'

I told him what I had discovered: Tanner listened with

eager eyes. When I quoted Mrs Dawkins' description, he gave an exclamation.

'Price, sir! It has to be.'

'Wasn't Mason once an employee of his?'

'Dead right, sir. It all fits. And what was it chummie said on that tape?'

'He said he might have to shop an old mate.'

'And that's what he's done, he's shopped Mason. He's been holing up with him here, and if Mason did Reydon, Price would know about it.'

I shook my head. 'But why would he shop him?'

Tanner stared. 'They might have had a row, sir.'

I said: 'First, he tried to steer us towards Saxby. He only came up with Mason when that didn't work.' I paused. 'Then there is the killing. Did it sound like the work of a mugger? A knife pressed to the throat will get you a wallet, no need to bury it in a man's back.'

'Then . . . what we've got here . . . ?'

'It begins to look like it.'

'Christ almighty!' Tanner said.

I said: 'We can't be certain yet. What happened here may have been an accident.'

'This wasn't any sodding accident!'

'Alternatively, Mason could have decided to end it himself. With his record, he would expect no mercy when he knew he was going to be shopped.'

'And Pricey brought him the booze to ease him through it?'

'According to Mrs Dawkins, they were both drinkers.'

'No, sir, no.' Tanner shook his head decidedly. 'If Price was going to shop him, Mason had to go. Price couldn't risk us talking to him, and all we should have found here was a corpse. Then we were supposed to call it off. We'd got our man, a convicted mugger. Too bad he'd beaten us to the punch, but that was that, end of story.'

155

I nodded. 'Just one other possibility. We may not be dealing with Price at all.'

Tanner gazed at me. 'Must be, sir. It all fits. It couldn't be any other.'

'Yet it's almost a year since he went bust, and that's a long time to meditate a violent revenge. And, as yet, we have no direct evidence that Price is involved at all.'

Tanner kept on gazing. He said: 'Just one thing, sir – Mason was supposed to die, and he didn't! And he's going to sing like a little canary when he comes round and hears what it's about.'

I said: 'If he comes round. We had better have a man there.'

'Yes, sir. I'll send one along right now.'

'Then we shall need a statement from Mrs Dawkins.'

Tanner ducked his head, and hastened out.

Five minutes later his team arrived to begin their work on the flat. I briefed them, then lit a pipe and strolled out on the gallery. Below, other figures had gathered to stare at the police cars, the flat, and across the way, on other galleries, or behind windows dimly lit. All of Ogden Street was alerted! And the missing man . . . where was he? I glanced at my watch. It was most of two hours since we had received that call at the police station. A man living rough . . . a dosser. Did he have some other hole to go to? Or was he perhaps, even now, somewhere below there, watching events: and preparing to vanish?

And for an instant I felt a strange rapport with that man, that fugitive with one, perhaps two crimes on his conscience: the voice on the phone, who – if it was he – had always sought to speak to me in person. Was he out there now, on the edge of some group, or perched in the shadow on a gallery: his eyes fixed on me as I leaned on the rail, drawing on my pipe? A man at the very end of his tether: a

156

man who could have no hope. A man terribly alone. Was it that I could sense his presence out there?

Tanner returned. He said: 'I've sent Thurloe to St Stephen's, sir. And I got them to ring through. They say Mason is still holding his own.'

I said: 'We need more men out there. There could be others with something to tell us.'

'Taken care of, sir. And the boys at the Court are giving Ikey Fischer's a going-over.'

I shrugged: if Price was our man, I doubted if we would find him in a place so obvious: better apply to the cardboard cities. But somewhere we had to start looking. I said:

'We need those men on the ground.'

Tanner said: 'I can't think chummie is still around, sir.'

'It's not impossible.'

But Tanner shook his head. 'He'd have been long gone, sir, before ever he made that telephone call.'

And that was the logic of it. Yet still I remained staring. Because was this a case where such logic applied? Once before chummie had taken similar risks, when he'd used a phone box only yards from the police station. Here, we weren't dealing with an average criminal . . . could he even be regarded as entirely sane?'

Two more cars homed in, and Tanner went down to brief the crews. A couple he brought back with him to knock on doors, the others moved away among the onlookers below. Tanner accompanied me back into the flat, where the scene-of-crime team were beginning to get results.

'It's the way you thought, sir . . . !'

They had located two distinct sets of prints in the flat, one of which occurred commonly, the other, so far, in three situations only.

'We tested the bottle, sir, like you told us, and there were this second lot of dabs all over it. Then we had a go at the door-handle, and found them there too. We tried the glass, but that was smeared and we couldn't get a good result. But there was another glass, in the sink, and we found the same dabs on that.'

'Were there any other prints on the bottle?'

'No, sir. Just those I said.'

Tanner's eyes glinted. 'The bastard!' he said. 'Not much doubt now what happened, sir. Chummie started off having a drink with Mason, and then he kept dosing him till he was pie-eyed.'

'When he turned on the gas.'

'Right. That bottle tells the whole story. Mason couldn't have been helping himself, he was having it dished up to him by chummie.'

'We shall need Mason's prints.'

'You bet, sir. And we've got chummie's for when we find him. Then we'll get a nice little tune from Mason, and that'll be the murderous bastard sewn up.'

'We still have to find him.'

'It shouldn't take long, sir. Not with the whole of the Met on his tail.'

'Also, we haven't tied him to the Reydon killing.'

'We've got Mason,' Tanner said. 'And Mason can do it for us.'

As though on cue, one of his men hurried in. He said:

'Sir, I kept in touch with the hospital, like you told me.'

'So what's the news?'

'I'm afraid Mason's had it, sir. He passed away without regaining consciousness.'

I left Tanner to do the swearing and borrowed a patrol car from out front. Without some exceptional stroke of luck, we'd got the guts out of Ogden Road. I could feel it in my bones: if the killer had lingered there, he wasn't lingering now: when the men on the ground had moved in he would have silently vanished away. And, meanwhile, I had another idea.

'Drop me off at Bertie's Hotel.'

It was late, but perhaps not too late, knowing the person I wished to talk to. And I was right. I found Bushell alone in reception, poring over the pages of a fat ledger. He gave me an interrogative stare when I entered, then nodded towards the private lounge. I said:

'Is she sober?'

Bushell grinned. 'Would you like me to find you up a chaperone?'

'Has it been like that?'

'She was even after me. But maybe she's cooled off a bit by now.'

I said I'd risk it, and went on in. I found Sara Lampard reclining on one of the benches. She must have fetched her clothes, since this evening she was wearing a sultry black number that showed more than mere cleavage. She was smoking a cigarette in a long holder, and had a half-filled glass on a table at her elbow; she flickered her eyelashes encouragingly as I approached, and patted the bench beside her.

'My favourite cop! I knew I'd score. Have you come to tell me you've locked up my husband?'

I shook my head.

'But wouldn't that be best? I mean before we wander up those stairs?'

'That isn't my purpose here, Mrs Lampard.'

'Oh, but how convenient it would be! Naughty Philip safely locked away while you and me . . . hmm?'

I sat down at a suitable distance, but Sara Lampard quickly closed the gap. Her eyes swam languorously towards mine, and she blew a puff of smoke over my head. She said:

'We haven't come to talk shop, now, have we? We've

come to help Sara forget all that. And I just love those
shoulders of yours. And that handsome face. And those
hands.'

I said: 'I've come to talk about men.'

'Oh darling, you've come to the right person!'

'About men you have known.'

'But there've been so many.'

'About one in particular. Joseph Price.'

Sara Lampard pouted. 'But couldn't that be later? I mean,
we've got all night, darling. If we really must talk about
other men we can do that in the morning.'

I said: 'I'm afraid it must be now. Did you know him?'

She said: 'You're not being very nice to me, darling.'

I said: 'Did you know him?'

She shrugged pettishly. 'But that was all such a long time
ago!'

'But . . . you knew him?'

'What – funny-face?'

'Joseph Price.'

Unwillingly, she nodded. 'He came to the house one day
with an invoice – well, I was feeling bored just then! I didn't
let it develop, darling, but I think I made an impression. He
hung around quite a while after that. But he wasn't a
handsome hunk like you.'

'He hung around?'

'I seemed to fascinate him. Some men can be such a pain.
But I only gave him that one little whirl. And in the end he
got the idea.'

'Was this before or after he went broke?'

'Oh, before. And only that once.'

'Have you seen him since?'

'Oh dear no. He ran away from his wife and kids, did you
know?'

'He ran away?'

'Skedaddled. Scarpered. And she was round here begging from Phil. A right little cockney madam she was, he gave her a handout just to get rid of her.'

'Where is she now?'

'Don't ask me, lover. She went back to her parents in Kensal Green. And funny-face was never seen again. So now do we get back to things that matter?'

I said: 'Thank you for your information, Mrs Lampard.'

She gazed into my eyes. 'You slay me, lover.'

I said hastily: 'I've a phone-call to make!'

Sara Lampard said: 'I'll be waiting for you . . . big boy!'

I escaped into reception and made my call from the desk. Edith had been left manning the office, but he had little fresh to report to me. A few witnesses had seen the man who had been staying at Mason's flat, but none could give any vital testimony, while the men who'd been searching the area had come up with a complete blank. I said:

'Give this priority. I want enquiries made at Kensal Green. We're looking for the wife of Joseph Price, said to be living there with her parents. Have you got that?'

'Got it, sir. Where do you want us to contact you?'

I fielded a wink from the grinning Bushell. I said: 'You can contact me at home.'

And so once more I returned to the scene of the crime, which happened to be also the place where I lived: near enough twenty-four hours later, one day since Reydon's body lay bleeding on the pavement. There was a light at Lampard's, but none at Reydon's: Anthea Reydon had presumably returned to her mother's; while Mrs Cartwright's milk-basket was put out, and the Mannerings' car had departed from our frontage. The pale spot was no longer visible: shadows lay in the access to the mews. On an impulse, I walked that way, and stood a moment absorbing the layout of the garages. That way the killer must have

161

come, there to be seen by the retreating car-thief: arriving by a footway from the Holland Park direction, and, beyond that, from Shepherd's Bush. Alarmed, he had fled the same way. Fled to the sanctuary in Ogden Road. But now that sanctuary had been sacrificed, and only the streets and the night remained to him. Did he know that his last, callous, fling had only drawn the noose about him yet tighter? I returned to the pavements, to the tree, and looked down the spoiled avenue of Lime Walk. Square at the end, where the eye fell on it, was the lighted window of Lampard's house.

'My dear, I have been longing for you to come! I am not your brave girl as I used to be.'

Fraught-faced, Gabrielle was in my arms even before the door had closed behind us.

'Have the Mannerings been gone long?'

'It is over an hour. Julia would have stayed on, but I would not let her. Only, my dear, that is not all. It is something that happens as they are leaving.'

'Something happened?'

'It is, perhaps, nothing, and you will say I am scared by trifles. I go outside to see them off, and wave as they are driving away. I am brave then, ha? But then I see him, I see this fellow standing in the alley, and there is something about him, I do not know, but I am flying inside and slamming the door.'

'A rough-looking man?'

She nodded. 'He is big and wearing a dark coat and hat. His face I cannot see. You do not think – it cannot have been him?'

I got Edith back on the phone; Gabrielle watched me with anxious eyes. I hung up. I said: 'It'll be all right now. There'll be patrols around here all night.'

'But, my dear, this is terrible! Why has he come back here?'

'It may not have been the man you think.'

'But yes. I am suddenly in fear. He is surely that man.'

I tried to calm her; I told her that an arrest was very near, that we were fairly certain of his identity, and that we had him on the run. But I doubt if she was listening; and at last she said:

'I do not know. This place is not the same, what has happened last night has changed everything.'

Then the phone went, and I knew, as I picked it up, what I should hear.

'Gently.'

'So you've got him, have you?'

Why did he have to breathe like that? I said:

'Listen to me, Price. Why don't you give yourself up?'

Just a moment of breathy hesitation, then:

'You go to hell!'

And the phone went dead.

11

As she proved on a famous occasion in the past, Gabrielle
has plenty of courage, is *une bonne fille de Rouen* with a touch
of Jeanne d'Arc in her make-up. But now the situation here
had grown acute, the horror of last night would not fade
away. It was continuing out there in Lime Walk, and had
just penetrated our very home. And she was right: it
changed everything. This familiar place had become un-
familiar. In twenty-four hours it had ceased to be our cher-
ished domestic base in London. Now, forced upon it,
would be memories that cancelled all those that went
before: the pale spot would refuse to fade, the figure of the
killer to vanish from the alley. By one loathsome act of
violence our residence there was being made untenable. I
said:

'You must go to Heatherings and stay there till we make
an arrest. After that, we will see. The lease here has not so
long to run.'

'But to this place we came when we were married!'

'Those are memories that no one can take away.'

'And, we have friends here.'

'We will still see them. Perhaps the Fazakerlys know of a
flat going in Chelsea.'

'But I do not wish to live in Chelsea. I wish to stay here, in
this dear flat.'

'Well, when you come back we will think it over.'

'Also, I do not wish to go to Heatherings.'

And she was stubborn: she wouldn't go; this nightmare wasn't going to drive her out. Did I not say there would be a police presence, and was it not arranged that Julia should spend the day with her?

'You could, perhaps, spend the day at Julia's.'

'Aha. And miss you, when you are calling here?'

'I may be kept away all day.'

'But I shall be here. And you will know where to find me.'

I suggested an intercept on our phone number, but even to this she would not agree. This man, this fellow, could breathe as hoarsely as he chose, and he would get one message – that he should give himself up. So at last, reluctantly, I gave in. Under police observation, she would continue at the flat. And, indeed, the argument seemed to calm her down, set her back on the pedestal from which, briefly, she had been shaken.

Before we went to bed I took a look outside, including a glance into the shadowy mews. But all was quiet, deserted. And the only light was a faint one in Mrs Cartwright's hall.

'We've got an address for Mrs Price, sir. Kensal Green were just on the phone.'

'Anything else?'

'Afraid not, sir.'

'Send me a car in half an hour.'

I lingered over breakfast, why not? The only lead we had wouldn't run away. The case was resolving itself, very largely, into a man-hunt, for which the odds had to be on our side.

Outside, I saw frost on the pavement, and a grey sky over the roofs. For the fugitive it must have been a harsh night, perhaps huddled in a doorway, or crouched under some bridge. Had he slept at all? Now the city was waking, with daylight probing his miserable refuge: the hunt was up. Surely it couldn't be long before he gave up a struggle so desperate?

'When is Julia due?'

In fact, she and the police car arrived together; I was able to leave her drinking coffee with Gabrielle, while proposing a descent on the local shops. Yet there was a fervour in Gabrielle's goodbye kiss, and a long look before I turned to go.

I found Tanner looking bleary-eyed. He said:

'That bugger has been on the phone again! He wanted to know if we'd got his old mate safe, said he didn't look so well when we carted him off.'

'So – he was there.'

'Yes, the cheeky sod. He must have hung around with the other riff-raff.'

'Then, later, he turns up in Lime Walk.'

Tanner shook his head wearily. 'He's a nutter,' he said. 'We're dealing with a nutter.'

'Who may or may not be Joseph Price.'

I told him of my interview with Sara Lampard. Tanner wasn't as struck as I thought he might be. He said:

'I've been thinking about what you said, sir. About it being a long time since Pricey took off.'

'Mrs Lampard may have offered an additional motive.'

'But that must have been longer ago still, sir. And Pricey just hasn't been around here. We'd surely have heard of him if he had.'

I said: 'We still need to turn him up. If his dabs don't match, then we can look further. And if they do, we have a case. Either way we need Joseph Price.'

'So like that we talk to the wife, sir?'

'We talk to the wife. At the moment she's the only link we have.'

Atlantic Court, the address we had for her, was a block of

council maisonettes. Neat, tidy, and with a well-kept grass plot, it looked a world away from Ogden Street. Mrs Price lived at Number 22. We parked, and Tanner rang the bell. The door was opened by a pert-faced brunette in her mid-thirties, clad in a house-coat and fur-lined slippers. She looked at us; then at the car. She said:

'If you want the sod, he isn't here.'

I said: 'May we come in, Mrs Price?'

'If that's what you want, I can't bloody stop you.'

We followed her into a bleak hall, and into a room where a vacuum-cleaner stood plugged to the wall. The furniture was cheap but fairly new. A child's desk stood pushed up into a corner. She turned to face us.

'So what's he done?'

'We are merely making enquiries, Mrs Price.'

'Go on, you're the second lot to come round here. That bugger has been up to something, hasn't he?'

I said: 'Have you seen your husband lately?'

She snorted indignantly. 'That's a laugh! The last time I clapped eyes on him was when he pawned my bloody necklace.'

'He pawned your necklace?'

'Yeah. The only decent thing he ever gave me. Said he had a bill to pay that couldn't wait, and I'd have it back at the end of the week.'

'And that was the last time you saw him?'

'Aren't I telling you? He'd flogged the car the day before. So he was on his uppers and I was trying to help him. But that's the last I saw of my bloody necklace.'

'When would that have been?'

'Last April, when we were living in Somerleyton Gardens.'

'Have you heard from him since?'

'That's likely, isn't it? When he left me and the kids without a sausage.' Mrs Price gave another snort. 'They

167

took the house and every damn thing. We were out on the street before you could spit. I had to put the bite on Phil Lampard just to buy food to feed the kids. So then my dad came and fetched us, and we was living with him for three months. Then he got me this place, he's on the council, and I'm trying to make a life for the kids here. Lovely, isn't it?'

'And you've had no news of him?'

'What bloody news should I have had?'

'No one has seen him?'

'Oh, that. Once, my brother thought he spotted him in Basildon.'

'In Basildon?'

'Kev is a rep. He was up that way in August. He was having his nosh in a pub, and thought he saw Joe in the bar. But if he did, then Joe saw him too, because he was out of there before Kev could speak to him.'

'And that was the only time?'

'Bar once, when Dad thinks he saw him at King's Cross. That was last month. Dad said he looked rough, could have been living in cardboard city.'

'Did your father speak to him?'

She shook her head. 'He'd just grabbed a taxi, he had to go.'

I said: 'Tell me, what sort of a man was your husband?'

She gave me a look, and her eyes were shrewd. She said: 'That bugger has done something, hasn't he? You haven't come round here just for the chat.'

'Would you say he was impulsive?'

'What, Joe? No. You always had to shove him to get things done. He was quiet enough, I couldn't complain. Not till the bastard let me down.'

'No violence.'

'I wouldn't have stood for it. But he was gentle enough with me and the kids. Just a big ugly sod. He was all right, before this.'

'A gentle man.'

'Yeah, I suppose. I don't know what he was like with the other blokes.'

'Gentle. Slow to anger.'

She stared at me. 'What are you getting at?'

I said: 'His business was hit by the recession, but he had this contract with the council. Then, at Easter, he lost that contract. Who was your husband blaming for that?'

'Well, it was bloody Phil Lampard who got it. But it was Reydon's who did the deal. And Phil was a bit of an oppo, I don't think Joe laid the blame on him.'

'So he blamed Reydon's.'

'I don't know. Why are you asking me this shit anyway?'

'Wouldn't he have discussed it with you?'

'Perhaps he did. But what's it about – what's he done?'

I paused, then said: 'We are making enquiries into the death of Stanley Reydon. At this stage our enquiries are incomplete, but we think your husband may be able to help us.'

The pert face paled. 'You're saying he did it?'

'At this stage our enquiries are imcomplete.'

'But . . . bloody hell!'

Mrs Price felt round for a chair, and sat down.

'Have you got the sod?'

I shook my head. She was staring big-eyed, her mouth drooping. Then her eyes switched to the window. She said:

'You don't think he's coming round here, do you?'

'Would that be likely?'

'How do I know! The bastard must be off his rocker, and if he finds out where I am . . .'

I said: 'You can count on a police presence. We are very anxious to interview your husband.'

'But if he comes here!'

'Then he will be arrested. You are unlikely to be in any personal danger.'

'But you don't know him.'

I shrugged, watching her. There was real panic in those staring eyes. She said:

'Listen, if he's round the bend, there's no telling what he might do.'

'But you say he is a gentle man.'

'That's just it! He's one of those quiet buggers you can't trust. You never knew what was going on behind that ugly mug of his. And if he's done what you said, then he must have flipped – and I may be next on his bloody list!'

'I repeat, I think it unlikely, Mrs Price.'

'And I'm telling you again, you don't know him.'

'Against Stanley Reydon he may have nursed a grudge.'

'Yes, and another bugger against me!'

I said: 'Did he blame Reydon?'

She snatched her head. 'Of course he did. That sod finished him off, didn't he? It was only the council job that kept us going.'

'Have you heard him threaten Reydon?'

'What he'd like to do to him. Though I never thought he meant it. How he'd duff the bastard up, if he ever met him on a dark night.'

'Duff him up?'

'Yes, what he said. And he's a strong, wicked sod who could do it.' She gave me a look. 'Is that what happened – he duffed him up, and went too far?'

I said: 'Perhaps you can help us, Mrs Price. Would you have any photographs of your husband?'

'Photographs – yes, I've got some! Though it's a wonder his bleeding mug didn't crack the camera.'

She fetched an album: and, for the first time, we were looking at the features of that elusive man, features so unusual, even grotesque, that for a while Tanner and I

170

studied them together in silence. A medieval face, harsh, square, with deep, straight lines in the granular cheeks, and a nose that wasn't only arched but ended in flaring, snubbed nostrils. The mouth was thin and wide, the eyes wrinkled and deep-set. It was such a face as one might have found carved on a corbel in some cathedral. Mrs Price watched us with a gleam in her eye.

'Wouldn't win any prizes with that, would he? And the sod has passed it on to Darren. But Kylie takes after me.'

'We would like to borrow a few of these, Mrs Price.'

'You can take the whole bloody lot for me.'

'Also, would it be possible that you have retained some of your husband's possessions?'

She gave her snort. 'You've a hope! In the first place, he never left anything worth having. And in the second, I slung everything away when we had to get out of Somerleyton Gardens.'

'You kept nothing?'

'Well – there was one thing. And I kept that because I give it to him myself.'

'And what was that?'

'His posh toilet-case. He had that on his fortieth birthday.'

'Would you mind producing it?'

I wasn't holding my breath yet, but I couldn't answer for Tanner. What Mrs Price handed me was a polished leather case with a lid secured by a zip. I stood the case on a table, unzipped it, and carefully opened the hinged lid. Inside were two silver-backed hairbrushes and silver-plated containers for shaving-brush and soap. I said:

'Has this been handled since your husband last used it?'

'Why should any sod want to do that?'

I said: 'Thank you, Mrs Price. We shall need this too. But it will, of course, be returned to you later.'

171

I gave her a receipt for the loot and, before we left, rang the local police station. For the next twenty-four hours, or until further notice, observation would be kept on Mrs Price's maisonette. It was perhaps unlikely that Price would show up there, or even that he was aware of his wife's address; but at least it reassured the lady, and left another stopped earth. Tanner was bubbling over as we drove away. He said:

'That's the first bit of luck we've had, sir! Just one dab on those blinking brushes, and we've got Pricey where we want him.'

'It still doesn't tie him in with Lime Walk.'

'Liddle, sir – we'll show him those photographs. That's all it needs, along with the rest. Liddle can nail him with the knife.'

'It would be stronger if he picked him out in an I.D.'

'And we might come to that, sir, before much longer. Price can't keep dodging us for ever, and he must be getting near the end now.'

'Meanwhile we'll take in Ogden Street on the way back, and see what Mrs Dawkins makes of the photographs.'

Ogden Street by daylight looked even more dismal than it did by night; the same cars, litter and graffiti, but enveloped now in a universal greyness. A single patrol car was parked there and we could see the two crew on the gallery; they appeared to be in conversation with Mrs Dawkins, and one of them was holding a ragged bunch of flowers. We parked and hurried on up.

'Sir, that chummie seems to have been back here! We found these stuck in the letter-box of the flat, and the lady says it was him who left them.'

The patrolman held out the bunch of withered flowers, which looked like discards from a florists'. Still dangling from the letter-box in the locked and sealed door was one unfortunate chrysanthemum.

'When was this?'

''Bout eight, it was.' Mrs Dawkins was looking tearful. 'I
see him through the window. I was just going to make a pot
of tea.'

'The same man?'

'It was him. He came creeping by, looking like the devil.
Then I heard him shove those in the door, and the next
thing he was off back again.'

I produced a photograph. 'Was this the man?'

She stared with moist brown eyes. 'Yeah, man, yeah.
That's just him. 'Cept he ain't so poncy as that, these days.'

'He must be daft as a brush,' Tanner said. 'Leaving flowers after what he's done.'

Mrs Dawkins began to sob. She said: 'It was decent of
him, man. Real decent.'

I looked at my watch. Three hours had elapsed since that
improbable tribute had been delivered. By now, our man
must be long gone, perhaps never to set foot in Ogden
Street again. Long gone . . . or was he? From the first, his
behaviour had been unpredictable. I eyed the street, the
blocks across the way, the lounging figures on the pavements. But then I shrugged. I said:

'We'll continue maintaining a presence here, and step up
patrols in the area. And Mrs Dawkins, if you should see
him again, I would be obliged if you would report it
immediately.'

Mrs Dawkins dabbed her eyes. She said: 'If he'm done
wrong, man, you got to catch him. But the flowers, that was
decent. He got to be a decent man somewhere.'

I showed the photographs to the fascinated patrolmen,
then we went down and got back in the car. Tanner called
in; within a short space of time, there would be small refuge
for our man in the Ogden Street neighbourhood. Tanner
hung up. He said:

'I can't think he's gone very far, sir! Not with the way he

173

keeps bobbing up. He must have kept hanging about here somewhere.'

'We can't house-search the whole district.'

'Perhaps he's holing-up with another mate, sir.'

'Do we know of one?'

Reluctantly, Tanner shook his head. 'But it might be a line to follow up.'

'So let's get back and have this toilet-case checked.'

'Right away, sir. But I've got this feeling.'

I had it too: it was almost a feeling that our movements were being watched, a feeling of the near-presence of this grotesque-featured man. Yet if it was so, he was staying invisible; as we slowly coasted down the street we saw no sign of him. Would it have to come to that mammoth house-search, with men drafted in from half the surrounding districts?

Edith was Tanner's dabs-man, and dabs there were on that convenient toilet-set. Edith lifted them, the comparison was made, and another nail driven into Price's coffin.

'Have these photographs copied and distributed.'

'What about Liddle?' Tanner said.

'Liddle can wait. We may grab Price.'

'But if Liddle –' Tanner began, when the phone interrupted him. Impatiently, he snatched it up, then, as he listened, his eyes grew wide. He snapped: 'Get some cars out there – quick!' He slammed the phone down and stared at me. I said:

'What is it?'

Tanner said: 'That bastard! He's had a go at Lampard.'

'At Lampard!'

'At his yard, sir. And that's only a step from Ogden Street.'

'Is Lampard hurt?'

'Just knocked about.'

'Come on,' I said. 'Let's go.'

174

There was an ambulance among the police cars pulled up in Hagg Lane, but we found Lampard still laid out in the lower office. He looked a mess, his face grazed and bruised, one eye closed, his clothes soiled and torn. One of the ambulance men was dabbing his cuts, but Lampard pushed him aside when he saw me. He gasped:

'It was him – it was bloody Price! You've got to put that maniac away.'

'How did it happen?'

'He was waiting for me. He jumped me in the wood-store.'

'You were alone?'

'I was checking a consignment. And there he was, behind one of the stacks. I said something, I don't know what, and then he was on to me like a tiger.'

'He knew you had recognized him?'

'Don't talk stupid! I knew him and he knew me. I was going to shout, but I didn't get a chance, the next thing I'd got a fist in my guts. Then he was punching me around as though he meant to make a job of it. He might have done, too, if Biggs hadn't heard him, but when Biggs showed up he took off.'

'Biggs?'

'My foreman. He'll tell you. If it hadn't been for him, I might have been a gonner.'

'That's right, sir,' a man in a boiler suit said. 'He'd got Mr Lampard down and he was kicking him and stamping on him. I shouted like crazy, and he cleared out fast.'

'Did you see where he went?'

'Towards the brick-piles. I called to some of the others to chase after him. Then I went to see to Mr Lampard, and me and another bloke got him across here.'

'Did you recognize the man?'

'It looked like Price, sir, but he was dressed pretty rough.'

175

'How long ago was this?'

'Not more than half an hour. I rang the police and the ambulance directly.'

Lampard felt his stomach, and groaned. 'He was out to do for me,' he said. 'The bastard. He never got over losing that contract. First it was Reydon, and now me. You'll have to get him.'

'We'll get him,' Tanner said. 'Don't worry yourself about that, sir. We've got the whole of the Bush sewn up. This time Pricey has been too cheeky.'

'He could turn up at my house –'

'We'll cover that, sir. I'll send a car round there now.'

'And then . . . who knows? There's Anthea!'

'Just take it easy, sir. We can handle it.'

I left him with Tanner and the ambulance man and strolled out into the yard. Certainly we had that covered: there were uniform-men near and far. I located the wood-store, one of the huge, open-ended asbestos-roofed sheds, and made my way through the stacks of timber piled high on either hand. I soon found the spot. Fresh smears of blood were apparent on the concrete floor, along with weals made by scuffling feet and other signs of violent disturbance. But had Price been laying in wait for Lampard? There was at least an alternative interpretation, namely that he had encountered Lampard accidentally, and attacked him to prevent his raising the alarm. And if that had been the case, what had Price been doing there? Why make for Lampard's yard, after leaving Ogden Road?

I stared at those neat stacks of timber, from which exhaled the resinous odour of pine. They were arranged in lanes and cross-lanes, filling the great shed almost entirely. Some of it was of recent delivery, some of it looked browner, older; while right at the end was a stack of something different, at a guess I would have said mahogany. I examined this stack. It was clearly of long standing;

dust had collected on the reddish slabs; here and there were the rings of tea-mugs, and burns attributable to cigarettes. And there was something else. An old door. It leaned against the blind side of the pile. Very quietly, I moved the door. The interior of the pile was hollow. Hollow, but not quite empty: it was furnished with sacking and a blackened pillow. There was also a bottle with a few dregs left in it, a crust of bread, and yesterday's *Standard*. Quietly, I replaced the door again, and went to fetch Tanner.

It was lunch time when we drove back to the police station, still without sign or word of the fugitive. But it was a somewhat less agitated Lampard who allowed himself to be carted off for a check-up. Clearly, his meeting with Price had been an unlucky chance, as much for one as for the other: Lampard had come out of it with a beating, while Price had lost probably his last bolt-hole. So now he was truly on the run, a man on the streets with no refuge. Derelict sites, alleys, doorways, they were his only resorts now. And everywhere eyes watching for him, his identity known, his description posted: while even the weather had turned against him: a few, mean, flakes of snow had begun drifting down.

'A fiver says we have him in a cell tonight, sir!' The finding of that bolt-hole had made Tanner jubilant. 'What do you say to us calling in Liddle, just to make it all neat and tidy?'

I shrugged: it probably wouldn't affect the issue, though an I.D. parade would have been stronger ground. I said: 'Have a proper card made up, and keep it strictly to the book.'

Liddle was fetched and sat down with the photographs, which included twenty of the most villainous mugs that

177

Tanner could lay hands on. There was no hesitation. When he came to Price, Liddle instantly picked out the card.

'That's the joker!'

I said: 'Can you be positive? He presents a very different appearance now.'

Liddle gave me a look. 'Are you kidding me, squire? I'd know that schnozzle out of a million.'

So that was it: Price was tied to the knife, tied to Reydon, tied to Mason: it remained a matter for the men on the ground, with help from the weather and a rumbling stomach. My part was almost played. I rang Gabrielle, but the telephone sounded in an empty flat. So I hung on, waiting for the break, for the moment of confrontation with that improbable phantom.

'We must have him soon, now, sir. We had the Bush covered before he could spit.'

'Yesterday, we nearly had him outside here.'

'But that was different, sir. He caught us on the hop.'

'Somehow, I don't think we should under-rate him.'

'Has to be human,' Tanner said. 'And the snow's coming down a bit harder. Any time now we'll get our tinkle.'

When the phone did ring, it was late afternoon, and the snow was dusting the lamp-lit pavements. Tanner took it, listened, then rolled his eyes, and handed the phone over to me. The same traffic sounds, the same breathing. I said:

'Price, why not call it a day now?'

I thought the breathing sounded harsher, but that was all. The caller hung up. I said:

'He's out of the Bush. I think that was just to let us know.'

'I'm going to have that sod,' Tanner said. 'I am.'

And he lit a fierce, a wicked cheroot.

178

12

Christmas came. We spent it at Heatherings, far from the
turmoil of the city. In spite of the early snow, it was a green
Christmas, even with a touch of spring about it. Hazel
catkins were out in a corner of the garden, and the birches
were purple above russet bracken. And the sea was a smiling blue sea that brushed the sands of the bay with spark-
ling white foam. We visited friends. Capel brought his
quintet to us, and we had a memorable evening of music.
Andy Reymerston presented us with a painting of Gabrielle's favourite view of the Walks. And there was no
news, not even the smallest, of the wanted man named
Joseph Price.

It hadn't been for lack of effort; his picture had been
released to the press, had twice appeared on BBC Crime-
Watch, to produce a rush of calls that led nowhere. A
general alert was in progress. Every police station in the
land displayed the Wanted poster. If Price was still among
the living, it seemed impossible that his arrest could be long
delayed. And yet, there was no news. It seemed he had
vanished from human ken. That bout of hoarse breathing
on the office phone appeared to have been our final contact
with Joseph Price. Tanner got grouchy if he was mentioned, and his underlings learned not to speak that name.

Christmas had improved Gabrielle's spirits, and for a
while I thought she had put the tragedy at Lime Walk

behind her. But then, when we returned from Heatherings, the shadow of it seemed to reach out to her again. The patch had gone, but not the memory. She sought to avoid going out after dark. When, as sometimes happened, I was absent in the evenings, she made hasty arrangements to entertain a friend. In the end I took a decision and got in touch with my relative-by-marriage, Siggy Fazakerly; there was, he thought, a flat falling vacant in the square where he lived, in Chelsea. I asked him to keep me advised, but for the moment said nothing to Gabrielle.

'Tonight, you will expect to be at home?'

I tried hard to manage my affairs so I would be. London just then was hell, the snow that missed us at Christmas had struck in January. With it came freezing fog and a spell of record low temperatures. My car I left in its garage, preferring the rigours of the tube.

'Tonight, you will expect to be at home . . . ?'

On one such night I was kept later than usual. It was past eight when I reached Kensington High Street, and the fog had come down long since. I'd rung Gabrielle. At the flat, I knew, there would be hot onion soup awaiting me. Head down, I crossed the road and hastened over snowy pavements towards Church Street. And then I hesitated . . . could it have been instinct? It seemed to me, suddenly, that I was being followed. I turned my head sharply, but could see no one, just the swirling fog furring the street lights. Other pedestrians were few, and even passing cars only occasional. I shrugged and hurried on. The fog, perhaps, was breeding illusions. But then again that feeling came to me – had I heard the scrape of a footstep back there? This time I stopped for a good hard look, but the result was the same, just empty fog. Very well then – if someone was playing games! I had learned to play them too. I strode on, ears alert, hearing now and then that scuffling scrape behind me.

180

I made my move at the turning into Lime Walk, reversing abruptly and darting back the way I'd come. I nearly ran into him: a black, looming figure, who staggered a pace backward at my sudden appearance. A bit of light fell on him from a street lamp. I saw that nose with the flaring nostrils. I saw the grained cheeks with the savage, straight lines, the colourless lips, the deep-set eyes. He was breathing hard, and shaking. Moisture was dripping from the nose. I had the impression that only a small shove was needed to send him sprawling in the road. I said:

'Joseph Price?'

His breathing had gone hoarse. Then a fit of coughing almost doubled him up. At last he croaked, in that graveyard voice:

'I've bloody had it. I've had enough.'

Then, because I was obliged to, I laid my hand on his wet, trembling arm, and said:

'Joseph Henry Price, I arrest you for the suspected murder of Stanley Reydon, also for that of Samuel Mason, and for grievous assault on Philip Lampard.'

He made no attempt to struggle. He croaked: 'Any use me saying I didn't do it?'

I looked into the grey, rheumy eyes, and slowly shook my head. He began coughing again, then he gasped:

'I meant to throw myself under a bus. I nearly did it. But I couldn't. And now I've bloody had enough.'

I said: 'When did you last have a meal?'

'Yesterday. I nicked a sandwich.'

'Not since then?'

'A couple of chips out of a carton someone had slung.'

I looked at him very hard. I said: 'Can I rely on you to come peaceably?'

'I tell you, I've had it.'

'I'm putting you on your honour, Price.'

'Just get me somewhere. Out of this.'

'Then come with me,' I said.

I kept my hand on his arm, and steered him up Lime Walk. He shuffled beside me like a zombie, his breathing noisy, his head sunken. We passed the spot on the pavement. I don't think Price noticed it. Then the tree. He gave no sign. Finally we came to my steps. I halted him, said:

'I want you to pull yourself together, Price. In the first place, wipe your nose. Then try to behave like a reasonable man.'

He used his sleeve, but at least he wiped it. He made a feeble effort to straighten his soiled coat. I pressed the bell, and the door opened at once; but poor Gabrielle's welcome died on her lips. I said:

'This is Price. He is under arrest. But I think he could use some of that onion soup.'

We got him into the lounge, where Gabrielle, without a word, spread a copy of *The Times* on the chair I was leading him to. Then she stood gazing at him, as though at a visitant from another world. And perhaps he was: a soiled, muddied bundle, with hair hanging down over his collar, a filthy hat and a filthy muffler hugging those strange, unshaven features, and sodden, cockled, muddied boots protruding from mud-glazed trousers. I said:

'You can take your hat off.'

Automaton-like, he obeyed. Also, he undid two buttons of the coat, and loosened the muffler from under his chin. It didn't improve matters, just altered the view. I looked at Gabrielle, the stare in her eyes. That first shock, that horror, had faded: had become ... wasn't it something like pity? After a moment, she went to fetch the soup, and I pulled up a chair, and sat. I said:

182

'You don't have to say anything, but anything you do say I'm obliged to report. Do you understand me?'

'Does it matter . . . now?'

Probably not; but he'd had his warning. I said: 'Do you want to talk about it?'

After a pause, he said: 'Sam.'

'Samuel Mason?'

'Sam. He was going to do it anyway. We both were, it was like that. Then I thought I'd hang on a bit longer.'

'And Lampard?'

'I had to do it. There wasn't any other way.'

'But to half kill him?'

'He had it coming. He knew what it would do if he cut me out.'

'So – you were after him too.'

'Just to rough him up. Like I only meant to nick Reydon.'

Gabrielle returned with a tray on which was a bowl we use usually for fruit, along with a baguette in a napkin and – because she was Gabrielle – the appropriate condiments. Price seemed bemused by it. But he started on the soup, and after several mouthfuls, tore off some bread. Gabrielle took a seat a good way from him. I said:

'I'll just step out and make some arrangements.'

Tanner wasn't there, but I got Edith, who told me that the fog was playing hell with the mobiles. I might have to wait for a patrol, but of course, he'd get a car to me as soon as he could. I told him to advise Tanner, and kept it brief. Price was still slurping soup when I returned to the lounge. Through a mouthful of soup and bread, he said:

'So what happens now, then?'

I said: 'You will be detained overnight in Kensington Police Station. In the morning you will appear before a magistrate, and after that be remanded to await trial.'

'Will you be there?'

'I shall be required to give evidence of arrest.'

183

'I mean – later?'

'If I am called. That will depend on the prosecution.'

He went on slurping a little longer. The soup had put a little colour in the grey cheeks. When it was finished, he ate up the bread, then wiped his mouth on the back of his hand. He stole a look at Gabrielle, at me; let his gaze fall back to the bowl.

'It was the woman,' he said. 'That's why.'

'The woman?'

'Why I did it. I only meant to cut him a bit.'

'Which woman?'

'Lampard's missus. I never meant to do the bastard in.'

After a pause, I said: 'You've had your warning. If you still want to talk, it's up to you. But in that case, perhaps we can go back to the beginning, and you tell me exactly what happened that day.'

He burped, then said: 'It was the day I came back here. I'd had to get out of Kensington, hadn't I? I cleared off. I was Basildon way. Then I ran out of funds. I was having to nick things.'

'So you came back here?'

'Not straight off I didn't. I hung out down east for a time. But things got worse, and the police were getting nosy. So I thought I'd slip back here and see the missus.'

'Didn't you know that your house had been repossessed?'

'Not then. I felt sure they would have let her keep it. It wasn't till I got back there, and saw another family in it, the kids in the garden. All that.'

'So what did you do?'

'I took off, didn't I? I couldn't ask at the police station where she'd gone. I roamed around till I came to the Court, to see what they were doing with my old yard. Perhaps you know what I saw there. It did something to me, something went. I swore I'd have his guts, Reydon. He'd done this to me. He'd have to pay.'

'Then you bought the knife.'

'That was after. When I came on this bloke just closing his shop. It was lying there in a box of junk, and I bid him a quid for it, all I'd got.' The deep-set eyes squinted at me. 'I wasn't sure then what I meant to do. But there was this knife, and I wanted it, so I bid him a quid. And he let me have it.'

'You armed yourself.'

'I'd got it. Maybe I'd use it, maybe I wouldn't. Perhaps I meant to cut him, just a little, just to make sure he'd never forget me.'

'You meant to use it.'

'To cut him.'

I heard a faint gasp from Gabrielle. I said: 'That was about six in the evening. What were you doing after that?'

'I went round to his place.'

'Straight away?'

'I saw him there. Saw him come out. He was on his own, he put the lights out. I saw him go down the street to Lampard's.'

'But you didn't attack him?'

'I couldn't, there were cars and people about. I had to have him on my own, and I knew I'd only have to wait.'

'You guessed why he'd gone there.'

'I knew.'

I said: 'Didn't you have a fancy for Sara Lampard?'

'Maybe once.'

I said: 'But still?'

He stared at the bowl with small eyes.

'So you waited. In Lime Walk.'

'I hung around. Near the house.'

'You were there all the time?'

185

'There's an alley to the back. I slid in there when people came by.'

'Did no one see you there?'

'Only one bloke. He came along feeling the handles of the cars. I knew what his game was. I drew off up the alley, but he came there too. I know he saw me.'

'And then?'

'I went back out. I kept close to that tree by the house. It was just after that when they came out, him and her, down at Lampard's.'

'You could see them.'

He kept staring at the bowl. 'She was hanging on like she'd never let go. And him, he was eating her up, with his hands over her backside. That was it. That's what did it. Seeing him and her together like that. I found I'd got the knife in my hand. But I don't remember a lot after that. I suppose I must have done it?'

'You stabbed Reydon.'

'I can't remember about that. It's like it happened to someone else, it's all a blank till I got back to Sam's.'

'Your knife was the weapon that killed him.'

'I heard someone shouting, and I ran. That's all I know.'

'There were three witnesses.'

'I never saw them. I don't know.'

His voice, which the soup had mollified, was becoming a croak again. I glanced at the tense-faced Gabrielle. She was sitting very upright, her hands clasped on her lap. I said:

'So you are claiming a degree of provocation.'

'I wouldn't have done it. Not except for her.'

I said: 'And after the stabbing, you sought refuge with Mason.'

'With Sam. I told you about him.'

'That there was a suicide pact.'

'We meant to do it. We'd got to the end, him and me.'

'But somehow, only Mason died.'

186

'He'd have done it anyway.'

'But you switched on the gas.'

He turned his savage face from mine. Soup was still clinging to the colourless lips. The eyes were deep, grey, hard, set under lowering, heavy brows. He said:

'What will I get?'

I said: 'It won't be less than life.'

'Then, like that, I could kill again.'

I just kept staring into those eyes. At last, his gaze dropped. He said:

'Well it can't be worse than out there! And I'm still bloody starving. Is there any more of that soup?'

Tanner came. He'd brought two cars, and Edith and Thurloe marched in with him. Tanner gave me a quick look, said:

'Sorry we're late, sir! Have there been any problems?'

'No problems.'

'Chummie is behaving?'

'He shouldn't give you any trouble. But – just to be on the safe side.'

Tanner laid his finger against his nose. He strode into the lounge, where Edith and Thurloe were already stationed, one each side of the prisoner. He stared fascinatedly at Price, then drew out handcuffs and hooked them on to Price's wrists. He grimaced as he stepped back. He said:

'You stupid beggar! Why did you have to leave it so late?'

Price didn't say anything. He was staring at his wrists, at the cold steel that now pinioned them. Thurloe picked up Price's hat and stuck it on his head. Then they marched him out, still silent, and manhandled him into one of the cars. Tanner said:

'I nearly had a fit, sir, when Edith told me you'd got him

here. I was thinking of the lady. It couldn't have been much of a joke for her.'

'Thank you, monsieur,' Gabrielle said. 'As a guest, this man was not expected. But he is such as my husband has to deal with, and it is fitting that I should have met him also.'

'But he was as rough as they come, ma'am. With Price, you were jumping in at the deep end.'

'He is bad, very bad, perhaps. Yet I am thinking he is human too.'

'Human, ma'am?' Tanner shook his head. 'All I can say is, it doesn't show through. But I'm glad you can put in a word for him, because where he's going he's going to need it.'

I briefed him with the details of Price's admissions, then he departed, and we were alone. Surprisingly, Gabrielle seemed able quickly to recover from the tensions of the last hour. She cleared away the tray, put *The Times* in the dustbin, and began setting out things for a meal. When I offered to help her, she waved me away. Like Tanner, I could only shake my head. At last we sat down, and then she said:

'I am glad. I am glad that man came here. It is for the best, do you not understand? Now I know he is a man, just like other men.'

'Not . . . quite like other men!'

'Perhaps. He has a face which is his misfortune. But underneath it, ha? Though he has done wicked things, he is a man like you or Inspector Tanner.'

'And that helps?'

She nodded. 'I think. Already things seem a little better. I am understanding what happened out there, it is a human thing. I begin to see it.'

I said: 'Reydon's sins found him out.'

'I am sad for that one, too.'

'And sad for Price?'

'He is yet a man. A man who is liking my onion soup.'

That night we didn't make love, just lay a long while in each other's arms. And the flat about us seemed more friendly, more the way it had been before that night in November.

Price collected a twenty-five-year minimum and received the sentence with no visible emotion. Shaved, trimmed and presentable, he looked several years younger, but no less remarkable or formidable. His wife attended the trial. Price ignored her. She took her revenge when she talked to the press. Another spectator was Sara Lampard, and once, just once, his eyes turned in her direction.

Anthea Reydon never returned to the house in Lime Walk. She sold the lease to an American company who needed a *pied-à-terre* for their London representative, an ebullient New Yorker called Hoffman, who perhaps cared nothing for an odd corpse on his doorstep. She herself moved to Knightsbridge, from where she continues to run the Contracts with flair and efficiency.

In April the flat fell vacant in Chelsea, but I indicated to Siggy that we were no longer interested. It wasn't that we had forgotten, or could ever forget, the tragedy that had occurred in Lime Walk. Simply, it had fallen into place, had become part of the tapestry of our lives there; but only a part: it had ceased to dominate the colour and fabric of the scene. Lime Walk had returned to its familiar variety, with this addition. And no more. Death had been absorbed by life: and so we kept our flat in Kensington.

Brundall, 1991/2

189